In Your Dreams

ROBIN JONES GUNN

BETHANY HOUSE PUBLISHERS
MINNEAPOLIS, MINNESOTA 55438

In Your Dreams
Copyright © 1996
Robin Jones Gunn

Edited by Janet Kobobel Grant
Cover design by Praco, Ltd.
Cover illustration by George Angelini

Scripture quotations are from the New King James Version of the Bible.
Copyright © 1979, 1980, 1982, by Thomas Nelson, Inc., Publishers. Used by
permission. All rights reserved.

Published by Bethany House Publishers
11400 Hampshire Avenue South
Bloomington, Minnesota 55438

Bethany House Publishers is a division of
Baker Publishing Group, Grand Rapids, Michigan.

Printed in the United States of America

Library of Congress Cataloging-in-Publication Data

Gunn, Robin Jones, 1955–
   In your dreams / Robin Jones Gunn.
      p.   cm. — (The Sierra Jensen series ; #2)
   Summary: While helping to care for her ailing grandmother and trying to
adjust to a new school and a new city, sixteen-year-old Sierra hopes that God
will bring something good into her life.
   ISBN 1–56179–444–9
   [1. Grandmothers—Fiction. 2. Old age—Fiction. 3. Christian life—
Fiction.] I. Title. II. Series: Gunn, Robin Jones, 1955–   Sierra Jensen
series ; #2.
PZ7.G972In   1996   96–25696
[Fic]—dc20   CIP
                                                       AC

04 05 06 07 08 09 10 / 24 23 22 21 20 19 18 17 16 15 14

To my sister-in-law, Kate Gunn Medina,
and her family: Al, Adrian, André, and Alyssa.
May Jesus ever be in your dreams.

chapter one

"*H*OW CAN YOU STAND TO LIVE LIKE THIS?*"* Sierra Jensen's sister, Tawni, snatched a pair of ragged jeans off the floor from her side of the room and hurled them onto Sierra's unmade bed. The jeans landed on a mound of clean clothes Sierra had removed from the dryer on Monday. It was now Thursday afternoon, but she had never quite found the time to put her clothes away.

"I'm not bothering your stuff!" Sierra said, grabbing the jeans and depositing them on the top of her dirty clothes pile on the floor. "Just because you're Miss Tidy Queen doesn't mean everyone else has to be like you."

"You don't have to be like me, Sierra. Just try to be normal."

"Normal! Normal? I *am* normal! You're the neat freak, Tawni. Never a blond hair out of place, never seen in public without makeup, never a chipped fingernail. Don't you ever get tired of living the life of a mannequin?"

"You are so rude."

"Oh, and you're not?"

"How am I rude?" Tawni challenged.

"You're throwing my stuff around. I'd call that slightly rude."

"I wouldn't have to throw your things around if you would clean them up once in a while. Like this weekend, for example. Do you think you could manage to keep *my* side of the room the way it is right now and try to clean up *your* side by Sunday night when I come back?"

Sierra bit her lower lip to keep her angry words inside. Letting them out never seemed to help. And the times she had, she regretted it later. But having to share her room with an older sister who was a clean nut had to be listed somewhere as one of the world's cruelest tortures. If she could find that list and show it to her parents, they would understand how much Sierra had suffered during her sixteen years of life with the perpetually perfect Tawni Sage Jensen.

"I mean it, Sierra," Tawni said, zipping closed her luggage. "You're going to have to give up your sloppy ways one of these days. I vote you start this weekend." Tawni turned with a swish and marched out of the room.

Sierra plopped onto the floor next to her pile of dirty clothes and took inventory of the surroundings. The two sides of the room couldn't be more opposite. Tawni's bed was made without a wrinkle, and her embroidered pillows were positioned on it just so. Her dresser was covered with a lacy, white cloth and set like a stage. Front and center was a slender vase with three red tulips picked from the front yard that morning. To the side were two porcelain frames, one containing Tawni's high school graduation picture and the other her baby picture. Each of her four bottles of perfume lined up in a row with their labels facing the audience. Perfume, or as Tawni called it, "fragrance," was her thing. She worked at a "fragrance bar" at Nordstrom. There she had accumulated a bunch of new friends, and this weekend they were going skiing at Mount Bachelor.

Sierra had plans for this weekend too. Not with friends, though. Since their family had moved to Portland a few months ago, Tawni had filled a page and a half in her address book with names and phone numbers of new friends. Sierra's address book hadn't seen the entry of a single name.

Making new friends was one problem, but an even bigger need was finding some spending money. Hopefully that would be taken care of soon. She had a job interview Saturday afternoon at a flower shop on Hawthorne, about seven blocks from the old Victorian house where they lived. Sierra liked flowers, but she wasn't sure she would catch on to how to arrange them. She had what she thought of as a different artistic eye than most people. This was evident by the way she dressed. Casual. Simple. Not on "display," the way

Tawni was with her appearance and her room.

That's how Sierra felt about herself too. Natural. Approachable. Her wild, curly blond hair flowed unhindered to her shoulders. Her blue-gray eyes, the shade of a winter morning sky, lit up her honest face. And the sprinkling of freckles across her nose had yet to be covered with makeup.

Sometime last summer, when Sierra was examining her freckles in the mirror, she had decided her best feature was probably her lips. They were equally proportioned on top and bottom. Round and full. Just right for kissing. But then, she wouldn't know. The only male who had kissed her smack on the lips lately was her three-year-old nephew, Tyler.

"Sierra?" A tap on her door followed Mom's voice.

Oh, great! Tawni told Mom to bug me about my room.

"Come in," Sierra said. "I already know what you're going to say."

Mom appeared in the doorway. Her normally calm demeanor was replaced with a frenzied look. She had on a straight, denim skirt, a white shirt with the sleeves rolled up, and she carried a slip of paper in her hand.

"What's wrong?" Sierra asked. "Are you okay?"

"Uncle Darren just called. Gayle's in the hospital. She and the twins were in a car accident. The boys are okay, but Gayle broke both her arms. I told Darren I'd try to catch the first flight out. There's one that leaves at seven tonight."

Sierra stood up, instinctively feeling she should

do something. "Is Aunt Gayle okay?"

Mom nodded. "Yes. She'll be in the hospital at least until tomorrow. But with both arms fractured, she'll be in casts for weeks. She obviously can't take care of Evan and Nathan. They were both asleep in their car seats when the other car hit them at an intersection. Darren says they're doing fine."

Sierra knew how close her mom was to her youngest sister, Gayle, and how Mom felt responsible to help Aunt Gayle in her time of need. Mom had gone to Phoenix eighteen months ago when the twins were born. She had taken on the role of mother to Gayle when their own mom had passed away twenty years ago, and now she had become a substitute grandma for the twins.

"Are you going tonight then? At seven?" Sierra asked.

"I need to talk it over with your dad when he comes home, which—" Mom glanced at her wristwatch "—should be any minute now. With Tawni off on her ski trip and Dad planning to take the boys camping this weekend, that would leave you home with Granna Mae."

"That's okay."

"I know you can handle everything," Mom said. "It's just that it can be tricky sometimes when Granna Mae has one of her memory lapses."

"I can handle it, Mom. She's almost always clear-headed with me."

Mom tucked her short, dark-blond hair behind her ear and gave a close-lipped smile. Sierra noticed her mom had nice round lips too.

"Are you worried about Granna Mae being home all alone tomorrow during the day? I could stay home from school, if it would help."

"No, you don't need to miss any school. I guess she'll be okay. After all, she managed for all those years by herself before we moved in."

"Mom," Sierra said, folding her arms across her chest. "I'm telling you it will be fine. Give me a chance to prove myself."

"You don't need to prove anything," Mom said.

Just then, Dad's footsteps pounded up the stairs. A moment later he appeared in Sierra's room. He was an energetic man whose receding hairline was the only hint that he was well into his fourth decade. "I heard," he said, giving Mom a quick kiss.

Sierra wondered if her dad ever noticed that his wife had lips shaped just right for the kiss he had given her. Do men even notice things like that? Especially after nearly twenty-five years of kissing the same lips every day?

"I can take a flight at seven," Mom explained, showing Dad the slip of paper. "Or there's one with a stopover in Los Angeles that leaves at 10:20 tonight."

"Take the seven o'clock. The boys and I will cancel our camping trip."

"You don't have to," Sierra said. "I'm staying with

Granna Mae. We'll be fine."

Mom and Dad exchanged hesitant glances.

"What?" Sierra said, stepping over a mound of her clothes and preparing to plead her case. "You guys are looking at me as if you think I can't handle this. Less than a month ago I managed to travel to England and back all by myself, remember? I think I can handle being alone with my grandmother for a few days."

"You're not the one we're concerned about," Dad said.

"Granna Mae has been fine lately," Sierra said. "Her memory lapse hasn't been a problem for the last week or so. Didn't she visit the doctor a few days ago?"

"Yes," Mom said, quietly closing Sierra's bedroom door behind her and speaking softly so only Dad and Sierra could hear. "He ordered some tests, and I took her in for them this morning."

"And?" Dad asked.

"I suppose the results will come sometime next week. Besides, what can the tests tell us that we don't already know? Her mind is slipping. Aside from that, she's in fine health."

"You guys can trust me," Sierra said. "She and I will be fine. Really." *And,* she thought, *it isn't as if I have to cancel my social life this weekend or anything, since I don't have one.*

Mom let out a deep sigh. "The boys have been looking forward to the camping trip. . . ."

"Okay. We'll go," Dad said in a quick decision.

"Sierra, you're in charge. Honey, I'll take you to the airport in an hour, and then the boys and I will leave on schedule at four-thirty tomorrow morning. Any problems, Sierra, you call Cody or Wes, okay?"

Sierra didn't think it was too practical to call either of her older brothers. Cody, his wife, Katrina, and their son, Tyler, lived in Washington, more than an hour away. And Wesley was going to school in Corvallis, almost two hours away. What good would they be in an emergency? She knew she could handle whatever problems might arise.

"You're incredible, Sierra. Did you know that? I never cease to be amazed by you and proud of you." Mom kissed her on the temple. "Oh, and by the way, if you find some spare time this weekend, you might want to straighten up your room."

chapter two

"SIERRA," A DEEP VOICE WHISPERED IN HER EAR. "Honey? The boys and I are leaving now." Sierra pried open her sleepy eyelids. "Dad?"

"Don't wake up all the way. I wanted to let you know we're leaving now. You have the alarm set, don't you?"

"Yes."

He planted a quick kiss on her cheek. "Thanks for holding down the fort. Remember, if you have any problems, call Mom at Aunt Gayle's, or call Wes or Cody."

"I'm sure everything will be fine," Sierra mumbled, snuggling deeper under the covers. "Have a great time. Catch a bunch of fish."

"We will. Bye, honey."

Sierra lounged a long time in that buoyant corridor between wake and sleep. Her fleeting dreams consisted of her sweet Granna Mae absentmindedly looking for a feather in the downstairs hall closet and her six-year-old brother, Gavin, teetering on the edge of a creek as a huge fish on the end of his line tried to pull him into the water. Then all of a sudden the missing feather fluttered onto an open page of Sierra's biology book. She reached over to pick it up and out of the corner of her eye spotted a figure wearing an Indiana Jones–style hat and a leather backpack.

She immediately opened her eyes. Only the dark shadows of her room greeted her. *Paul.* Letting out a deep breath, Sierra closed her eyes and tried to go back to sleep. She wanted to fall into a deep sleep, where fragmented dreams have room to dance like crazy and then disappear with the morning light. That's where Paul belonged. In her dreams.

The next two and a half hours she wrestled with the covers, trying without success to fall back to sleep. At seven she finally rolled out of bed in a bad mood and stumbled into the bathroom for a shower. She wasn't sure if she should wake Granna Mae or simply leave a note saying she had gone to school and would be back around four.

After deciding on a pair of baggy jeans (which Tawni thought looked ridiculous) and an embroidered peasant blouse (which Tawni thought was pathetic), Sierra took a long look in the full-length mirror at the end of the upstairs hall. She was glad Tawni couldn't force her fashion advice on Sierra today.

She heard Granna Mae stirring in her room. Sierra gently tapped on the door.

"Come in, Lovey!" This was a good sign. Granna Mae's nickname for Sierra was "Lovey." It had also become a clue as to whether Granna Mae was operating in this time zone or not. If she didn't refer to Sierra as "Lovey," she might be thinking Sierra was someone else from another era in Granna Mae's life. This morning Sierra harbored fears that Granna Mae's mind might slip into its precarious time machine and transport her mind and soul into another time frame.

"Good morning," Sierra said cheerfully as she stepped into the large bedroom.

Granna Mae was making her bed, pulling up the thick down comforter and covering it with her favorite old handmade blanket. It was a patchwork collection made from squares of fabric she had kept over the years from clothes she had made for her children. The bedroom was cheery and charming, with a window seat in the rounded window alcove and a fireplace that was used often.

"I'm almost ready to leave for school. What are you going to do all day?" Sierra asked.

"Oh, I thought I'd do the usual: go roller skating this morning and bowling this afternoon. There might be time to take tea with the mayor before you come home." The mischievous twinkle in Granna Mae's eye let Sierra know she was spry this morning and her usual self.

"Sounds fun," Sierra teased back. "Be sure you wear your elbow pads."

The phone rang, and Sierra reached for it on the nightstand before Granna Mae could make it around to that side of the bed. The large green letters on the digital clock read "7:58." Sierra needed to leave for school in two minutes.

"Is this Mrs. Jensen?" the male voice on the other end asked.

"This is Sierra Jensen, Sharon's daughter."

"I was trying to reach Mrs. Mae Jensen."

"Oh, she's right here." Sierra covered the mouthpiece with her hand and said, "It's one of your boyfriends. Probably wants to add bungee jumping to your list of today's activities."

Granna Mae took the phone while Sierra finished making the bed. She heard her grandmother say, "Oh, yes. Good morning ... Oh ... Oh ... No ... Okay ... Yes ... Well, no ... Okay. Good-bye." She hung up the phone just as Sierra was scooting out the door.

"So?" Sierra called over her shoulder. "What are you going to do today? Bungee jumping or skydiving?"

"I'm having my gall bladder taken out," Granna Mae replied.

Sierra laughed at her grandma's quick wit. "Well, have fun!" She bounded down the stairs and reached for her backpack off the hall tree by the front door. "Have a great day!"

"Oh, Sierra," Granna Mae's high-pitched voice called from the top of the stairs, "could you give me a ride?"

Sierra stopped in her tracks, irritated that she would be late for school now. She often drove her grandmother to the pharmacy or the grocery store, but why couldn't her grandma's errand wait till Sierra came home? "I'll give you a ride wherever you want to go as soon as I get home."

She was about to close the door behind her when she heard, "But I need to be there before nine."

"Before nine this morning or nine tonight?"

"Nine this morning," the twittering voice replied.

Sierra stepped back inside the house and tried not to sound irritated. "Where do you need to go?"

"The hospital."

Now Sierra knew something was off in Granna Mae's thinking. "Not today, Granna Mae."

"Yes, today," she said. "This morning. Dr. Utley said I shouldn't drink or eat anything and to be there by nine o'clock. I can call a cab." With that she turned at the top of the stairs and padded back to her room.

"Okay," Sierra called after her. "I'll see you around four this afternoon."

"I won't be here. I'll be at St. Mary's Hospital. You can come directly there to see me."

How could her grandmother's mind slip so suddenly? Sierra didn't know what to do. She couldn't leave Granna Mae like this. She might actually call a cab and have herself carted off somewhere. Then what would Sierra do if she came home and Granna Mae wasn't there? With a frustrated huff, Sierra dropped her backpack on the floor and took the stairs two at a time. She found Granna Mae in her room, neatly

folding some of her underclothes and tucking them
into an overnight suitcase.

"He said nothing to eat or drink, not even water.
And now I'm hungry, just because I know that. It's
such a good thing Dr. Utley checked the test results
this morning. He's leaving today at three and won't
be back for a week. I can't wait that long." Granna Mae
reached for a bottle of lotion and kept chattering as
she packed her hospital bag. "So that's why I don't
mind going in on such short notice. I want Dr. Utley
to do the operation, of course. He's the one who took
out Paul's appendix."

Paul was one of Granna Mae's sons. He had been
killed in Vietnam, and his death had left a heavy mark
on Granna Mae. Whenever she started to talk about
Paul, she had almost certainly dipped into la-la land.

"Well, I tell you what," Sierra said, sitting down
on the edge of the bed. She reached over to touch her
grandmother's hand and thus coax her to stop pack-
ing. "You wait right here at home today. Right here in
your room. You'll be just fine here. You can watch
some TV or read a book. And when I come home,
we'll go see Dr. Utley together. How would that be?
Would you like that?"

Granna Mae gave Sierra an irritated look and
calmly withdrew her hand. "I don't know why you are
speaking to me that way, Sierra Mae Jensen. But let
me tell you right now that I am completely serious.
That was Dr. Utley on the phone. The test results show

that I must have my gall bladder removed right away. If I want him to do the operation, I must go in this morning. Now don't you worry about a thing. You go on to school. I don't need a ride. I'll call a cab."

Sierra didn't know what to believe. And she didn't know what to do.

"I . . . I can stay a bit longer," Sierra said, deciding she would wait out this waking hallucination with her grandma and go to school as soon as she knew Granna Mae was thinking clearly again.

"Oh, dear!" Granna Mae said, looking at the clock. "It's 8:25. I've made you late for school, haven't I, Lovey?"

Sierra froze. *She called me Lovey. She's never called me that unless she's thinking in the present. What if she's telling the truth?*

With her mind scrambling at a furious pace, Sierra popped up and said, "That's okay. Why don't you finish up here? I'm going downstairs for a few minutes." She closed the door behind her and raced down the stairs to the study. In the top drawer of the old rolltop oak desk was the phone book. Sierra pulled it out and frantically flipped the pages until she found Dr. Utley's number. She dialed, and the minute the receptionist answered, she said, "Yes, I need to talk with Dr. Utley right away. It's very important. My name is Sierra Jensen."

"One moment, please."

The moment felt like an hour as Sierra waited.

She could hear her grandma's footsteps upstairs in the bedroom right above her. "Come on, come on!" she breathed into the phone.

"Dr. Utley speaking."

"Yes, hello. My name is Sierra Jensen, and my grandmother is Mae Jensen. I'm sorry to bother you, but she thinks that you called her this morning, and that she's supposed to have an operation. But, you see, I don't know exactly what to believe because her mind sometimes plays tricks on her and—"

"I see," the doctor said, interrupting her. "Is your mother there?"

"No," Sierra said. "I just wondered if you'd mind talking with her and setting her straight."

"Actually," the doctor said, "I think you're the one I need to set straight. Your grandmother had some tests yesterday, and her regular doctor sent me the results. She has several gallstones. One has escaped from her gall bladder and is clogging her bile duct. I've scheduled her for surgery this morning at eleven. She needs to be at the hospital by nine."

Sierra felt as if someone had sucked all the air out of the room. "Okay," she finally managed to say. "I'll take her right away." She hung up the phone and took a deep breath. Her heart pounded.

"Lovey," came the calm, birdlike voice from the stairs, "I'm ready to go."

chapter three

S<small>T. MARY'S HOSPITAL WAS ONLY A FEW MILES FROM</small>
Granna Mae's house. Sierra found a parking
place near the entrance, and they checked in at
the front desk at ten minutes before nine. Granna Mae
had to sign papers, and then they were sent up the elevator to a room where Granna Mae was instructed to
change into a hospital gown and wait on the bed.

"I'll be right back," Sierra said, thinking this would
be a good time to call her mom.

"Not yet, Lovey. You need to watch the door for
me. I don't want one of those male nurses barging in
here while I'm changing."

Sierra drew the curtain around the bed and stood
watch by the door. She had to stop a lab technician.
"She's changing," Sierra explained. "It'll be just a
minute."

"Is that Ted?" Granna Mae called out.

Sierra bit her lip and felt her heart pounding at
top speed again. Ted was Sierra's grandfather. He
had died when she was a toddler. This time Granna

Mae *had* to be confused.

"My name's Larry, ma'am. I need to take a sample of your blood. You let me know when you're ready for me."

"I'm ready," the calm voice replied.

Sierra drew back the curtain. Granna Mae was in the bed with the white sheet pulled up to her chin. She had an innocent, passive look on her face. The sparkle she had exhibited earlier that morning was gone.

"Make a fist for me," Larry said as he reached for her creamy white arm. "A little poke here.... Hold on, I'm almost finished. ... There. Bend your arm and hold this right here."

Granna Mae didn't flinch. She glanced at Sierra and smiled. *Oh, my dear Granna Mae! Who do you think I am when you look at me? One of your daughters? A nurse? Do you even know I'm here? I wish I knew what to do!*

For the next hour Sierra didn't leave Granna Mae's bedside. They didn't talk much. At least Sierra didn't talk much. Granna Mae asked for things like a blue scarf she said she had left in the car and a cup of coffee. She wanted to know what time they were leaving. None of it made sense. Sierra agreed to everything but didn't move.

Granna Mae didn't seem to notice. She willingly signed a form listing all the items she had brought to the hospital. She went to the bathroom when the nurse told her to, surrendered her arm for the IV, and only winced slightly when the needle was inserted. In a way,

Sierra was thankful for the cushion of illogical thought that padded her grandmother's preparation for surgery.

When it came time to wheel her off, Sierra asked if she could speak briefly with the doctor.

"Come with us," the nurse advised. Sierra followed her, walking alongside Granna Mae's rolling bed. Impulsively Sierra reached over and grasped her grandma's hand, squeezing it as they moved down the corridor. Granna Mae's hands were elegant, silky white, and softly wrinkled.

"Do you mind waiting here?" the nurse asked.

The hospital bed was wheeled forward, and Sierra reluctantly let go of Granna Mae's hand. "Bye," she whispered.

A moment later, an older man dressed in mint-green hospital garb approached Sierra. "Are you Mae's daughter?"

"Granddaughter," Sierra corrected him. "Yes, I'm Sierra. I wanted you to know that she's a little confused. She was fine this morning, after you called, but now she seems mixed up. I don't know if that makes any difference with the surgery, but I wanted you to know."

"I appreciate it," he said, patting Sierra's hand. "Don't worry. She'll be fine. Will you be able to sit with her in the recovery? I think it would help her to see a familiar face when she wakes up."

"Yes, I'll be here."

Sierra felt a huge knot tightening in the pit of her stomach. She knew she had to call her mom and let her know what was happening. But dozens of obstacles were in her way. First, she didn't know Aunt Gayle's phone number, and she didn't know if she should go home to find it or stay nearby while Granna Mae was in surgery. She decided she shouldn't leave the hospital.

Maybe the best thing would be to call her brother and his wife. They would have the number, and they could call Mom.

Sierra scrounged through the bottom of her backpack and found she didn't have enough money to make the long-distance call. She would have to phone collect. Katrina would understand.

The only problem was Katrina wasn't home, and the operator wouldn't let her leave a message on the answering machine. So there she was, with no money and no further along in her quest. Her only choice was to go home.

Once inside the big, empty house, Sierra went about placing her phone calls. First, she phoned Aunt Gayle's, where she left a message on the machine. She didn't want to freak out Mom by telling her Granna Mae was in the hospital. All she said was, "Hi, it's Sierra. Mom, when you have a chance, could you call home today … right away. I need to talk to you." She hung up and wondered if the message should have been more urgent.

Jotting down the number, Sierra tucked it in her backpack and decided to try to call later from the hospital. Then she punched in Cody's number again and left a message on his machine for him to call her at home. Again, she didn't mention Granna Mae or the operation.

Sierra grabbed a carton of orange juice, a couple of granola bars, and all the spare change she could find in the kitchen drawer where Mom kept her stash. It was mostly coins recovered in the dryer, which Mom claimed were her "tips."

Then Sierra hurried back to the hospital, where she waited for nearly two hours. Twice she tried Aunt Gayle's, but each time she hung up right before the answering machine picked up on the call so she could retrieve her change. She didn't know what else she could do but sit and wait for Granna Mae to be released from surgery. It seemed like the slowest couple of hours in her life.

At about 1:30 a nurse came into the waiting room and told Sierra she could be with her grandmother in the recovery room. There, in a straight-back chair, Sierra waited another few hours, half dozing, half flipping through a few magazines. She thought she should try to call Mom again but didn't. What if Granna Mae woke up while she was gone?

Sierra pulled out the last granola bar and took a chomp. Just then she heard a low groan.

"I'm right here," Sierra said, hopping up and standing beside the bed. Something inside her welled up and made her want to burst into tears. Her sweet grandma looked so helpless, lying there hooked up to all those tubes. She gently reached for Granna Mae's hand. "It's okay," Sierra said, as much to comfort herself as Granna Mae. "You're going to be fine."

A nurse came in and went about her duties as Sierra stepped to the side. "I'll be right back," Sierra said. "If she says anything, tell her Sierra will be right back."

She scooted down the hall to the pay phone and tried Aunt Gayle's number. It was busy. She waited a few minutes and tried again. Still busy. It made her nervous, as if she was going to get in trouble for bringing Granna Mae in for surgery without asking anyone's permission.

She tried the number again. This time it rang. She assumed someone was there and let it ring four times, but the answering machine picked it up after the fourth ring.

"Hi, it's Sierra again. Mom, I really need to talk to you. Ummm. . . . " She didn't know how much she should say. "I, uh . . . ," she stammered. Then fearing that she might run out of time to leave her message, she blurted out, "I'm at the hospital and Granna Mae—" Before she could finish her sentence, the machine beeped loudly in her ear and cut off her sentence.

"Oh, great," she muttered, fumbling to find some more change. All she had was thirty-five cents. Not enough to call Phoenix. Feeling exasperated, Sierra hurried back to the recovery room to check on Granna Mae. But when she got there, Granna Mae was gone.

chapter four

"*E*XCUSE ME. I'M LOOKING FOR MAE JENSEN. Do you know where they moved her?" Sierra asked.

A uniformed nurse with a clipboard scanned her list and said, "Room 417. The elevator is at the end of the hall."

Sierra breathed a sigh of relief. For a moment she had feared something had gone wrong, and they had taken her grandmother back into surgery.

Sierra stepped calmly into the elevator and decided she had been watching too many hospital shows on TV lately. Room 417 was in the middle of the hall near the nurses' station, and Granna Mae appeared to be sleeping soundly when Sierra entered.

Granna Mae had a distinctive snore. It was faint and steady, a sort of ruffling of the air.

Sierra stood beside her and spoke softly. "It's me, Sierra. Are you feeling okay? I prayed for you. I'm sure everything went just fine."

Just then Dr. Utley stepped into the room and

asked, "Has she awakened yet?"

"Not really. Not all the way."

"She'll probably sleep for the next few hours. The anesthesia has most likely worn off by now, but she's on some pretty strong painkillers, and those tend to cause drowsiness." Dr. Utley looked closely at Granna Mae's face and did a quick scan of the IV and catheter tubes. "She looks good. I'm sure she'll be fine. We were fortunate we spotted the problem when we did. She only had two gallstones, but they were both large. I had to make an incision about six inches long right here." He traced his finger across his abdomen, under his right rib cage.

Sierra resisted the urge to clutch her stomach. She felt queasy just hearing about the surgery and decided she didn't want to see the incision.

"I'll need to keep her here about a week. She'll be pretty groggy the first few days, but it will help her to know you're here." Dr. Utley smiled at Sierra. "You do know, don't you, that your grandmother is a remarkable woman?"

Sierra smiled back. "I've always thought so."

"It wouldn't surprise me a bit if she bounced back from this in half the time of most patients her age."

Sierra lowered her voice, just in case Granna Mae could hear her. "It makes it even more difficult to see her body still strong but her mind . . ." She trailed off, not sure how to complete that sentence.

"I know," Dr. Utley said, nodding his understanding.

"A little patience and a lot of love go a long way." He glanced at his watch, and then with a renewed spring in his voice said, "Well, I have a plane to catch and a very long overdue vacation waiting for me. I've assigned my associate, Dr. Adams, to take over for me. He will probably stop by sometime this evening."

"Thank you," Sierra said. "And have a great vacation!"

"I plan to," he answered on his way out the door.

Sierra moved closer to the bed and tried to talk to Granna Mae again. "Did you hear that? Dr. Adams will be checking in on you. I'll stay as long as you want me to. If you need anything, you just tell me, okay?"

When Granna Mae responded with a slightly deeper snore, Sierra settled into the upholstered corner chair. She tucked her legs up underneath her and looked out the window. The room faced another row of hospital rooms. Four floors down, in the center of the complex, was a lush garden. It was raining, and in the sky above, streaks of dark gray clouds seemed to be dropping lower while another layer of lighter gray clouds appeared fixed in place, blocking out the blue sky. A typical spring afternoon in Portland.

Sierra thought about all that had happened to her during the past few months. In January she had gone to England on a missions trip. She had become close friends with three of her roommates, Christy, Katie, and Tracy. Even though they were older, Sierra felt she fit in with them just fine, better than she fit in with most people her own age. While she was in England, her family had moved to Portland from a small mountain community in northern California. In Pineville, Sierra had known everyone, and everyone knew her. She was one of the most popular girls in her high school. Here, she was nobody.

Going to a Christian school in Portland had seemed like a good idea because it was so much smaller than the public schools and therefore more like the high school she had attended in Pineville. But after returning from England, Sierra found it hard to settle back into her junior year. She started off poorly, and although things had leveled out, she still hadn't connected with any of the other students. Of course, a lot of it was her fault. She hadn't worked very hard to make friends. But still, it was a Christian school, and she would have thought the students would be more friendly to her than the mobs at the public school. It didn't seem to be turning out that way.

Granna Mae stirred, and Sierra peeked over at her. She settled back into a rhythmic snore, and Sierra went back to daydreaming out the window.

Sierra knew she had to keep her appointment for the job interview at the flower shop tomorrow, even though she felt as if she shouldn't leave Granna Mae. Without the job, she had no spending money. Without the spending money, she would never break into the circles of students at Royal Academy.

One time, some of the girls had invited her to go

out for pizza on a Friday night. Sierra had agreed to go, but when Amy came by to pick her up that evening, her parents weren't home to ask for money, and Sierra didn't have even a dollar in change.

Amy seemed to understand when Sierra used the excuse of not being able to clear going out with her parents. But that was two weeks ago, and Amy hadn't invited her to do anything again. Sierra felt certain the job would be the key to her social life.

For hours she sat listening to Granna Mae's breathing, greeting each nurse who slipped in to check on the patient. Sierra's stomach began to grumble, and she thought she should go home to find something to eat and to try to call Mom again. But she didn't want to leave until Granna Mae had awakened enough to know Sierra was there.

Finally, when it was growing dark, she gave in. Sierra stopped at the nurses' station and explained that she would be gone only an hour or maybe even less. They smiled but seemed absorbed in their routine and not nearly as concerned about Granna Mae as she was.

It felt strange walking up the dark steps of the old house and unlocking the front door. She had never been there by herself. In a family of six children, she had rarely been home by herself. It gave her the creeps to step into the silent entryway and grope for the light switch on the wall.

The smell comforted her. It was a subtle mixture of cinnamon and mothballs. The scent hinted at childhood memories of her favorite hiding place during a game of hide and seek, the great, deep downstairs hall closet with the fuzzy red and yellow wallpaper. She would scrunch up in the back corner behind the winter coats and draw in that mothball, cinnamon fragrance.

One summer her dad had read a story to them about four children stepping through a closet full of old coats and entering a magical land called Narnia. Sierra believed it could really happen. As a matter of fact, she was convinced that Granna Mae's closet was equally enchanted, and if she entered it at just the right time, she too would be transported into Narnia. She had tried many times, up until about the age of eleven. Even though she stopped trying, in her heart, she still believed.

It was a wonderful dream, and one she wished she could surrender to right now. How comforting to curl up in that closet. But she was sixteen and responsible for her grandmother's welfare.

The first thing Sierra did was try to call Mom again. This time her uncle answered. "Hi, it's Sierra."

Before she had a chance to say another word, her uncle started to shout into the phone. "Where are you? What is going on? What was that phone message all about? Sharon, come here! It's your daughter."

Uncle Darren had never been Sierra's favorite.

Sierra's mom spoke into the phone. Her voice sounded calm in a forced way that told Sierra her mother was stressed. If Mom was home now, she would put on her jogging clothes and run until she was good and sweaty. "Are you okay, Sierra?"

"I'm fine. It's Granna Mae. This morning Dr. Utley called and said the test results showed she needed to have her gall bladder out immediately. He did the operation at eleven this morning."

Mom listened calmly as Sierra gave the details. Sierra could hear Uncle Darren breathing heavily, listening in on the extension. That bugged her. As soon as she finished, Uncle Darren said, "We've been trying to reach you all afternoon. Do you know what you've put your mother through?"

"It's okay," Mom said quickly. "How is she?"

"She was still sleeping when I left. I'm going back as soon as I eat something. Mom, do you know if there's any money around here? I had to raid your dryer tips to find enough change to call you."

Mom directed Sierra to an envelope taped to the inside of one of the desk drawers in the study and told her to take as much as she needed. Sierra pulled out twenty dollars.

"I'll see what I can do about coming home tomorrow," Mom said.

"Oh, great," Darren muttered and hung up his extension.

Mom was quiet for a minute before saying, "Things are a little rough here. Do you think you'll be okay by yourself for the night?"

"I'm going back to the hospital. I want to stay with Granna Mae all night."

There was another pause before Mom said, "You're a mother's dream, Sierra. Do you know that? Call me if anything at all goes wrong, okay? Even if it's the middle of the night. If I don't hear from you, I'll call the hospital early tomorrow morning."

"Okay. That'll be fine. I'm sure she's going to be all right," Sierra said.

"That's what I'll be praying," Mom said.

chapter five

SIERRA SPENT THE NIGHT CURLED UP IN THE corner chair of Granna Mae's hospital room. Sometime around 3:30 in the morning, Granna Mae woke up. She moaned terribly and sounded as if she might be crying.

Tumbling out of the chair, Sierra went to her grandmother's bedside and quickly pressed the call button for the nurse. "It's okay, Granna Mae. The nurse is coming. Do you want a drink of water?" Sierra reached for the cup at the bedside and offered Granna Mae the straw. But she didn't drink. She didn't open her eyes. She only groaned and tried to move.

"Where is that nurse?" Sierra muttered. "Are you uncomfortable? Can I help you move or something?"

The nurse entered the room. "Yes?"

"She's groaning," Sierra said, trying not to sound as frantic as she felt. "I don't know what to do."

"How are you doing there?" the nurse said, gently lifting Granna Mae's hand and taking her pulse. "Are you having some pain?"

Granna Mae only moaned louder.

"We can give you something for that." She checked the IV bag and said, more to herself than to Sierra or Granna Mae, "And we'll hang another bag of fluid for you."

"Does she know I'm here?" Sierra asked the nurse.

The nurse nodded. "She's just groggy. It's good that you're here. Keep talking to her. I'll be right back."

Sierra reached for Granna Mae's hand and held it gently. It felt cold and clammy. "How's my favorite lady?" Sierra asked brightly. Cheering up the elderly and the sick wasn't Sierra's thing. But Granna Mae was her favorite lady, and she would do anything for her—even act brave when she felt queasy.

Granna Mae settled back to sleep after the nurse took care of her, and Sierra returned to her blanket and her curled-up position in the chair. Sleep didn't return to Sierra's mind or body. During the chilled, hazy hours of the early morning, she thought and prayed and thought some more.

The phone jarred her from limbo-land sometime after seven o'clock. Sierra jumped to answer it.

"Hi, it's Mom. How are you doing?"

"I'm fine. Granna Mae had a pretty good night. She's still sleeping," Sierra whispered into the phone.

"No, I'm not, Lovey. Who is it?"

Sierra looked over at Granna Mae. Her eyes were puffy, but she was obviously awake. "It's Mom. Do you want to talk to her?"

"I suppose. Not much to say." Her voice sounded low and raspy.

Sierra held the phone next to her grandmother's ear.

"No, I'm fine," Granna Mae said, apparently in answer to Mom's question. "I don't think I can move, though. They have me all wired up here."

As Sierra watched, a cloud seemed to move over Granna Mae's face like the clouds Sierra had observed out the window yesterday afternoon. Dark gray streaks of confusion began to gather in Granna Mae's eyes. She looked up at Sierra and then at the phone.

"Tell them I don't want any!" Granna Mae snapped. She turned her head away from the phone and tried to inch her shoulder away.

"Mom?" Sierra quickly pulled the phone to her ear. "I think she's a little confused."

"I just don't want any," Granna Mae muttered. "If I wanted another dish towel, I would have told them."

"Mom?"

"It's okay, Sierra. You just stay calm and steady. It'll be all right. Listen, I'm at—"

Sierra dropped the phone and reached for Granna Mae's hand. She had started to tug at the IV tubes, trying to pull them out. "You need to leave that there," Sierra said firmly. "You can't take this out yet." She wrapped one hand around Granna Mae's wrist so she couldn't pull out the tube and hunted with the other hand until she found the call button for the nurse.

From the dangling phone receiver she could hear her mom calling to her. "There you go," Sierra said, patting Granna Mae's hand and gently pushing it away from the IV. "You're okay."

"But I don't want it!" Granna Mae squawked. "They should have asked me!" Then she started to cry like a little girl with all the fight drained out of her.

The nurse stepped in. It was a nurse Sierra hadn't met yet. "Hi," Sierra greeted her nervously. "She's trying to take out the IV."

"Naughty, naughty," the nurse said, half teasing and half sounding as if she was scolding a toddler.

It made Sierra mad. "Hey," she said defensively. "She doesn't completely understand what's going on, okay?"

The nurse gave Sierra a startled look and reached for Granna Mae's free hand to take her pulse. Sierra cautiously let go of the hand with the IV and retrieved the phone. "Mom?"

"I'm right here, honey. Is everything all right?"

"I don't know. I think so. She just sort of clouded over and ... "

"You did the right thing. Listen, I was trying to tell you that I'm calling from the airport."

"In Phoenix?"

"No, I'm in Portland. I took the first flight out this morning. Do you want me to grab a cab to the hospital?"

Sierra hesitated. She knew it would take only half

an hour to drive to the airport and back to the hospital. "No, I think she'll be okay. I'll come pick you up." Sierra kept a keen eye fixed on Granna Mae and on the nurse. "I'll meet you out in front of the baggage claim."

She hung up and watched the nurse as she entered some data on the wall computer where all notes and medications were logged. Granna Mae appeared to have slipped back into a restless sleep.

"I'll be right back," Sierra said to the nurse. "Please keep an eye on her."

"That's what I get paid the big bucks for," the nurse said in a snippy tone.

Sierra dashed out of the room and wished she had told Mom to take a cab after all.

Easing the little Volkswagen Rabbit out of the hospital parking lot and scooting down the freeway toward the airport went smoothly. But the tricky part was making sure she took the right exit. Sierra had gotten lost more than once on the freeways around Portland, and this morning she didn't have any time to spare. She felt so responsible for Granna Mae.

The sign for the Portland airport loomed ahead of her, and she pulled into the turn lane with no problem. She found Mom in front of the baggage claim and hopped out to give her a hug.

Sierra felt like crying the moment Mom's arms encompassed her. But she refused to give in. She had been strong this long, so she could be strong for Mom too.

Mom chucked her luggage into the back of the car, and Sierra slipped into the passenger seat. She let out a sigh of relief as they exited the busy terminal area. In more than one way, Mom was now in the driver's seat.

"How are you doing?" Mom asked, shooting a sideways glance at Sierra. Before she could answer, Mom added, "I wish we could contact your father. Did the doctor say how long she would be in the hospital? Has she eaten anything yet?"

"Fine, I don't think so, and no," Sierra answered, using her brother Wesley's approach of answering Mom's string of questions. Sierra hoped the technique would lighten the situation.

Mom smiled. "I don't even remember my questions. I've been so concerned for you both. Let me start over. Are you okay?"

"Sure. I'm fine."

"I'm proud of you, Sierra."

"I didn't do anything. Actually, Mom, I almost blew it." Sierra told her about not believing Granna Mae at first when the doctor called.

Mom shook her head. "I'm glad you had the sense to stay home. I don't know if I would have. Do you want me to take you home so you can sleep?"

"No, I'd like to go back to the hospital with you." Sierra glanced out the window as they entered the freeway. That's when she remembered her job interview at ZuZu's Petals that morning at nine. "Actually, maybe I better go home so I can shower before my interview. I'm feeling a little bit crumpled."

"You'll have to walk to your interview then," Mom said.

"That's fine. It's only a few blocks."

At five minutes to nine, Sierra was feeling like her "few blocks" had turned into a few miles. She hoofed it a bit faster, grabbed a handful of her wild, curly blond hair, and flipped it up and down. It was still wet underneath. She had on a gauze skirt that hung a few inches below her knees and her favorite footwear, her dad's old cowboy boots. As unique and beat-up as they were, those boots were Sierra's good ol' buddies and her trademark. She wore a long-sleeved T-shirt covered by an embroidered vest.

A light drizzle followed her down Hawthorne as she trekked the final block to the flower shop. She passed a bakery, buzzing with locals waiting in line for hot, fresh Saturday morning cinnamon rolls. The door opened, and a wonderful blast of cinnamon assaulted Sierra, beckoning her to join the others in line. She knew she didn't have time if she was going to keep her nine o'clock appointment at ZuZu's Petals, three doors down.

In twelve long strides, she was there. Sierra breathed a quick prayer and turned the knob on the large wooden door. It was locked.

chapter six

*S*IERRA PEERED THROUGH THE SIDE WINDOW OF the flower shop and gently tapped on the glass. The lights were off inside, and she didn't see anyone stirring in the back room.

This is bizarre. I know the interview was for this morning. It's after nine. Why isn't anyone here?

She looked around, thinking maybe the owner had gone out for a cup of coffee or one of those hot cinnamon rolls. Sierra reviewed the phone conversation she had had with the owner a week ago. She was sure the time had been set for this morning at nine.

Granna Mae was the one who initially had arranged for the interview. She loved flowers, and for years ZuZu's Petals had been "her" florist. More than once Sierra had heard Granna Mae say, "If I had two dollars, I'd use one to buy bread and one to buy flowers. Bread may feed the body, but flowers feed the heart."

Granna Mae had called ZuZu's Petals last week to order flowers for one of Sierra's aunts back East who had just had a baby. Before her grandmother had hung up, she had handed Sierra the phone and said, "They'd like to hire you, Lovey." The appointment was set up in a few sentences, and now Sierra stood in front of the vacant shop wondering if the whole thing had only been in her dreams.

An older man and woman walked by in the steady morning drizzle with cups of coffee in their hands and a white bag that probably held cinnamon rolls. "Good morning," they said in unison to Sierra.

She smiled and returned the greeting. Two women strode past her, caught up in lively conversation. A short man leading a huge black dog on a leash trotted right after them. Sierra felt like a hotel doorman, standing at her post under the green canopy of the shop's front door. Her taste buds were shouting, "Get a cinnamon roll!" Her logic was droning out all the reasons she should stay put and wait for someone to show up. Her stomach was constricting with the thought she should have gone back to the hospital with Mom and rescheduled this interview. For a full twenty minutes she stood in place.

At last a white minivan pulled up in front of the shop and parallel-parked. The words "ZuZu's Petals" were painted in fancy pink script on the sliding side door.

"Are you Sierra?" the driver asked, hopping out and sprinting to join Sierra under the protection of the awning. "I'm Charlotte. Sorry to keep you waiting."

She unlocked the door and flipped over the closed sign. "We had two huge weddings to deliver this morning. Come on in. Would you like some coffee?"

"No, thanks."

"So, you're Mae's granddaughter. She's a favorite of mine. How is she?" The energetic owner had very short, black hair and snappy dark eyes to match. In her right ear she had at least six silver earrings. Sierra hadn't decided yet if she liked her or not.

"Well, actually, she's in the hospital. She had her gall bladder removed yesterday."

Charlotte stopped in her tracks and looked at Sierra, horrified. "She's okay, isn't she? I had no idea! Is she at St. Mary's?"

"Yes. She seems to be doing all right."

"Are you going to see her today? I'll send some flowers with you. I got some gorgeous daffodils in yesterday. I'm so sorry to hear she's in the hospital!" While Charlotte rapidly gave her condolences, she poured herself a cup of coffee behind the counter and opened a small refrigerator with her foot. In one motion she grabbed a carton of French vanilla–flavored coffee creamer, poured it into her cup, returned the carton to the refrigerator, and closed the door again with her foot. "Sure you don't want some coffee?"

"No, thanks."

"I live on this stuff!" Charlotte said, whirling around and flipping a switch that turned on all the lights in the charming shop. Sierra wondered how much of Charlotte's vivaciousness came naturally and how much was caffeine-induced.

"Okay," Charlotte said, boosting herself onto a stool behind the cash register and taking a sip from her ceramic mug. "The pay is minimum wage, the hours are Saturday and Sunday, eight to five, and you need to use your own car, but we'll reimburse you for gas and mileage. Do you want the job?"

Sierra stood there, stunned. *That was my interview?* "I'll work Saturday all day, but I can't work Sunday, and I can't guarantee I'll always have a car. I thought you were looking for someone to work here at the shop, not run deliveries for you."

"Nope. I need a gofer. That's why I was out this morning; my two associates are still out. The three of us need to run the shop. We're looking for someone to do the deliveries. And Sunday is part of the package deal. I'm not interested in hiring you if you can't work both Saturday and Sunday."

"Then I guess this won't work out," Sierra said just as directly as Charlotte was being with her. "Thanks anyway. I hope you find someone."

She turned to go, and Charlotte called out, "Wait!" She hopped off her stool and hurried into the back of the shop. A moment later she returned with a huge bunch of bright yellow daffodils mixed with long-stemmed blue irises all wrapped in green paper with a pink bow. "For Granna Mae. Tell her we all send our best."

Sierra received the bundle of flowers. The only way to carry them was like a beauty queen, cradled in her arms. "Thanks. She'll really appreciate these."

"I know," Charlotte said, reaching for her coffee mug. "See you around, Sierra."

Stepping out onto the wet sidewalk, Sierra wished she had an umbrella. The light rain was steady now, and although she didn't mind getting a little wet, she felt the flowers should be protected. It was an unusually large bouquet, beautiful but a little overpowering. The awkwardness of toting such a bundle made Sierra change her mind about waiting in line at the bakery for a cinnamon roll. It was all she could do to carry the flowers. Anything else in her arms would surely meet with disaster, especially in the rain. She passed the bakery, promising her taste buds she would be back one day soon.

The rain was coming down hard now. Sierra wished she had worn a jacket. Her T-shirt clung to her arms, and her skirt stuck to the back of her legs. She could feel her hair drooping down her back and adhering to the sides of her face. A chill swept through her as she walked even faster, trying to protect the innocent bouquet from getting soaked. She felt miserable.

All her emotions seemed to have collected into one big bundle, and Sierra felt fifty pounds heavier carrying them home with her in the rain. She hadn't gotten the job. She still had no money, no social life, no hint of things getting better in the near future, and her dear

Granna Mae was in the hospital and slowly losing her mind. The calm, steady days of her family's predictable life in Pineville were over. Community picnics, horses, and fields of wildflowers were exchanged for crowded neighborhoods with barking dogs, pollution-belching buses, and flower shops run by quirky people amped out on caffeine. Sierra felt terribly alone.

Then, because she thought it would help her feel better, Sierra let herself cry. Big, fat tears rolled down her cheeks, feeling hot in contrast to the chilling rain-drops that joined them. She tilted her face to the sky and let the cool rain wash over her. Sierra felt little sieges of sobs tremor inside her chest. She didn't care who saw her or what the people who passed her on the sidewalk thought. A few whimpers escaped her lips. She didn't try to stop them. Nothing in her life seemed to be going the way she thought it should.

The rain poured over her. She felt as if she had been doused with a bucket of water. Only five more blocks to go, and she would be home where she could crawl into bed. Or better yet, into a hot tub.

Sierra came to a stoplight and had to wait before she could cross the street. Out of the corner of her eye, she noticed a black Jeep that had come to a stop at the red light only a few feet from her. Even though the windows were rolled up, she could hear the beat of the music blasting from the Jeep radio. She also heard laughter. Male laughter. Deep and rowdy laughter. She couldn't help but wonder if they were laughing at her.

And she couldn't blame them if they were. She probably would be laughing at the sight of her if she was the one in the Jeep. Sierra knew she must look ridiculous, like a runner-up in the Miss Drowned Rat Beauty Contest.

The sound of their laughter only added to the hurt already coursing through her. It made her mad. Sierra blinked away her tears and, with a jerk of her head, glared at the insensitive males inside the Jeep. The guy in the passenger seat was looking right at her. Their eyes met. Sierra stopped breathing. The grimace on her face vanished. And the guy in the passenger seat stopped laughing.

It was Paul.

The light changed, and the Jeep jerked forward as Paul turned his head to get one last look at Sierra. Then he was gone.

She put one foot in front of the other, sloshing into a puddle as she crossed the street. Everything inside and outside had gone numb.

It was Paul. He saw me. He was laughing at me.

Sierra barely remembered the final blocks home. Her mind had been transported back to the phone booth at Heathrow Airport in London where she had met Paul. He had asked to borrow some change for his phone call, and somehow, something inside of Sierra and inside of Paul had connected. They spoke later on the plane and found they had mutual friends. It was all very promising. Then he found out how old she was. He was a big college student, and she was only a junior in high school. His interest in her seemed to evaporate. But then he wrote her a letter, and she answered it. That was several weeks ago, and he hadn't written back. Now, after this morning's curbside encounter, she was sure he never would. It was one more thing to cry about. And cry she did.

chapter seven

SIERRA STRETCHED OUT HER LEGS IN THE WARM water of the antique cast-iron tub. She hadn't soaked in the claw-foot tub since she was a little girl visiting Granna Mae during summer vacation. After her family had moved to the old Victorian house, she had taken showers in the upstairs, remodeled bathroom. Now she sank deeper into the soothing water.

The minute she had reached home, she had called the hospital. Mom said Granna Mae was resting and doing fine. Then Mom suggested Sierra get some sleep to make up for the restless night she had spent in the hospital room chair. After lunch, they could go back to the hospital together.

The leisure time was just what Sierra needed. A nice hot bath, a change into old sweats, and a cup of jasmine tea lifted her emotions out of the bog that had entrapped them an hour earlier.

Just as Sierra was pouring her second cup of tea, the phone rang. "Hello," she said. A far-off part of her heart hoped it would be Paul.

"Hey, Sierra! Whatcha' doin'?" the female voice asked.

"Not much. Who's this?" It drove Sierra crazy when people started to talk before she knew who they were.

"You mean you've forgotten us already?" the voice teased.

"Hi, Sierra," another female voice chimed in. "It's Christy. I'm sure you can guess the other mystery caller."

"Katie? Christy! Hi! How are you guys?"

"We're peachy," Katie said. "How about you?"

"That's her new word," Christy interjected. "I guarantee you'll get sick of it real fast."

Sierra pulled the tea bag out of the mug and headed to the office with the remote phone balanced on her shoulder. She curled up in her favorite chair and placed the hot tea on a coaster on the end table. "I'm so glad you guys called! It seems like years since we were in England."

"I know," Katie agreed.

"But it's only been a few weeks," Christy pointed out. "What's happening with you?"

"Don't ask!" Sierra warned, sipping her tea. "It's been a not-so-happy couple of weeks topped off by a couple of disastrous days. You guys tell me about you first. Maybe it'll cheer me up."

"Well, we're baking cookies right now," Christy said. "At least we're trying to—if Katie will stay out of the chocolate chips."

"I only had a handful," Katie responded. "Besides,

48   IN YOUR DREAMS

if we add raisins, no one will know the difference."

"Todd will," Christy said.

"Is Todd there too?" Sierra asked.

"No, he's at his dad's in Newport. We're going there this afternoon because Tracy is having a party at her house tonight. We really wish you were going to be at the party, Sierra."

"Don't taunt me like that. You know I would love to be. I would give anything to see you guys again!"

"So come on down," Katie said in her best game-show-host voice.

"Oh, right. There is this little matter of the thousand or so miles that separate us."

"Ever hear of airplanes?" Katie asked. "Marvel of the modern world. You could be here in a few hours."

"Ever hear of money?" Sierra said. "As in, I don't have any?"

"Then get some," Katie said.

"I tried." Sierra tucked her feet underneath her to keep them warm. "I had the world's fastest job interview this morning, and I didn't get the job. It was for a flower shop. They wanted me to work all day on Sundays and use my own car for flower deliveries."

"Did you tell them you couldn't work Sundays because you go to church?" Christy asked.

"No. She didn't even ask why. I just told her I couldn't work on Sundays."

"I used to work at a pet store," Christy said. "My boss understood when I told him I couldn't work

Sundays because I went to church. Maybe you could try explaining it to her."

"It doesn't matter," Sierra said. "I don't have a car. My mom and I share an old beater that's not so dependable. I know I couldn't take it for the whole day even if they just hired me for Saturdays. It wouldn't work out."

"That's too bad," Christy said. "Are you going to apply anywhere else?"

"There are plenty of shops and fast-food restaurants around where we live. I'm sure I'll find something."

"When you do," Katie advised, "be sure to tell them you can't work during Easter vacation because you're coming down here to spend the week with us."

"If I get some money."

"You have to. It's mandatory," Katie said.

Sierra heard a low munching sound in the phone. "Katie, are you eating those chocolate chips again?"

"Just a few."

"Katie," Christy said, "we're going to have to buy some more. I never thought I'd say this, but maybe that health food kick you were on wasn't so bad. At least every bit of chocolate didn't disappear when you were around."

Sierra laughed. "I'm so jealous of you two."

"Jealousy is not a good thing," Katie said.

"You know what I mean. You've been best friends for all these years. Since we moved here, I haven't found anybody I could even ask to come over and make cookies."

"You'll find someone there soon," Christy said.

"Oh yeah? How?"

"Advertise," Katie said with a crunch.

"What?"

"Put a classified ad in the school newspaper."

Sierra laughed. "What would I write? 'Wanted: Kindred Spirit'?"

"That would work," Katie said with another obvious munch. "What could it hurt?"

"Where do you come up with these ideas, Katie?" Christy asked. "And stop eating those chocolate chips!"

"Didn't you know that chocolate is the best brain food on planet earth? It heightens one's awareness of the obvious. And it's obvious Sierra needs a soul mate, and I still think advertising is the way to go."

"I'll be praying God brings a wonderful, peculiar treasure right to your door," Christy said.

"She's not ordering a pizza," Katie pointed out. "Take my advice, Sierra. Advertise. It's the best way. Very peachy. But speaking of peculiar treasures, and peachy peculiar treasures, what happened with Paul?"

"Funny you should mention him," Sierra said.

"Who's Paul?" Christy asked.

Katie explained in one long breath. "Remember that guy I told you about that Sierra met at the airport in London on the way home, and he just happened to be a Christian and just happened to be on the same flight and just happened to know Doug because his brother, Jeremy, and Doug are close friends, and when I went down to Doug's last month, Jeremy was at the God Lovers' Bible Study and gave Doug a letter from his brother to give to Sierra, and Doug gave it to me, and I sent it to Sierra."

"You never told me any of this," Christy said.

"Of course I did!"

"No, you didn't. I would have remembered."

"I'm sure I told you, Christy. You seem to have a selective memory lately."

"And what is that supposed to mean?"

Sierra sipped her tea and listened to her friends rant with each other on their long-distance call to her.

"If it has to do with Todd, your memory is perfect. Anything else is up for grabs lately."

"Oh, that's real nice, Katie. Thank you very much. The point is, you never told me about Sierra meeting this guy . . . what's his name?"

"Paul," Sierra and Katie said in unison.

"And I saw him today," Sierra inserted quickly, before Christy and Katie had a chance to continue their friendly spat.

"How peachy! Tell us everything," Katie said.

Sierra recounted the drowned-rat-with-extra-large-bouquet scenario. There was complete silence on the other end except for the rustling sound of a bag of chocolate chips.

"Hello? Did I bore you two to death with my story?"

"Of course not," Christy said. "It's just weird, your seeing him like that. What are you going to do?"

"Nothing. What can I do?"

"Maybe he'll call you to see if you're okay," Katie said. "That's what happens in the movies."

"No," Christy said, "in the movies he would have told his friend to stop the car, and he would have run back to you with an umbrella and walked you the rest of the way home, and you would have made a pot of tea."

Sierra laughed. "I am drinking tea right now," she said. "Maybe my life is a low-budget 'B' movie, and all I get is the tea. No hero. No umbrella."

"Yeah, well then my life is a class 'Z' movie," Katie said. "No hero. No umbrella. No tea. No plot—"

"Yours is more of a mystery," Christy interrupted cheerfully. "The ending will surprise all of us."

"And your life," Katie said to Christy, "is turning into a rather predictable romance. Girl meets boy. Boy is a dork for four years. Girl blossoms into a gorgeous woman. Boy finds his brain. Girl turns into starry-eyed mush head."

Sierra laughed. "I take it things are still going great with you and Todd."

"Slightly," Katie answered for Christy. "You have to hurry down here, Sierra. I'm calling an emergency meeting of the Pals Only Club. Since you and I are the only remaining members, you are obligated to come. You do remember our club, don't you?"

"How could I forget?" Sierra said. "I do have to

say I still qualify for membership. No guys are in my life—not even as pals." Then, because she was feeling rather perky, Sierra added, "Unless Paul was actually so taken with my ravishing appearance this morning that he's on his way here even as we speak, so he can sweep me off my feet."

"In your dreams!" Katie said. "I'd say you can check that loser off your list. Maybe your ad should be for new members of Pals Only; we could even add some guys to our tiny band."

"Don't advertise," Christy advised. "Just start praying. I'm going to pray that you'll meet some fun people up there."

"Then start to pray that I find a job. Easter vacation is only three weeks away."

"I will," Christy promised.

Just then the front door opened, and Sierra jumped. She wasn't expecting Mom until this afternoon. The antique clock on top of the oak desk read 10:57. Sierra listened to the footsteps on the wood floor in the entryway. She wished she had locked the front door. Cupping her hand over the phone, she said, "You guys, somebody is in the house."

"Are you the only one home?" Christy asked.

"Yes," Sierra whispered back, feeling her heart pound faster as the footsteps headed toward the kitchen. They sounded heavy, like a man's. "Don't hang up. Stay on the line. If you hear me scream, call the Portland police immediately!"

chapter eight

SIERRA HELD HER BREATH. IN THE PHONE RECEIVER she could hear Katie slowly smacking her lips, and Christy whispering, "Katie, shhh!" With her other ear, Sierra listened as the footsteps clomped through the kitchen and seemed to come closer.

"He's coming into the study!" Sierra whispered.

"What's happening?" Katie whispered. "Who is it?"

A figure suddenly appeared in the doorway. "What are you doing here?" Sierra demanded.

Tawni marched in, her heavy snow boots thumping across the polished wood floor. "What are *you* doing here?" she asked. "Where's the car? I didn't think anyone was home, and I couldn't figure out why the front door was unlocked."

"Who is it?" Katie shouted into the phone.

"It's my sister," Sierra said. Then turning to Tawni she said, "Mom has the car. She's at St. Mary's with Granna Mae. She had her gall bladder out yesterday."

"Who?" Tawni squawked. "Who had her gall bladder out? Mom or Granna Mae?"

"Yeah," Katie chimed in, "you didn't tell us this!"

"Granna Mae. Mom came home this morning to be with her. She's doing okay."

"Who?" Katie asked. "Your mom or your grandma?"

"Both," Sierra said. "Can I call you guys later?"

"We'll be down at Tracy's tonight. You can call there," Christy suggested. "Or we'll try you again in a week or so to see how things are working out for you to come down at Easter."

"Okay, great. Bye, you guys. Say hi to Doug and Tracy and Todd for me!"

"We will. Bye, Sierra."

She hung up and faced Tawni, who had her hands on her hips. "What is going on?" Tawni demanded. Sierra repeated the information, and Tawni said, "I'm going to the hospital."

"I'll go with you," Sierra said, hopping up. "Let me put on some shoes."

"I'm going to change, and then we'll go," Tawni said, leading the way up the stairs in her ski apparel.

"What happened with your ski trip?" Sierra asked. "I thought you were staying until Sunday."

Tawni opened their bedroom door and shouted, "Sierra!"

"What? I'm standing right here!"

"This room looks as if it hasn't been touched since I left on Thursday!"

"It hasn't, Tawni. I was slightly busy. What happened with your ski trip?"

"Nothing!" Tawni snapped. "I decided to come home early, that's all. It looks like it's a good thing I did. How did you manage to get Granna Mae to the hospital?"

"I drove her."

"You ditched school?"

"I *missed* school." Sierra pulled on some warm socks and slipped her feet into a pair of tennis shoes. "It was an emergency."

Tawni didn't have a real cheerful personality, and she often got mad at Sierra, but today she seemed more irritable than usual. Sierra chose not to push her sister for an explanation as to why she had come home early.

Tawni changed her clothes in silence, neatly hanging up her ski jacket and arranging her boots in the corner of her closet. They walked downstairs with Tawni in the lead. Sierra grabbed her backpack, which was still wet from her walk that morning, and was about to lock the front door behind her when she remembered the flowers in the kitchen sink.

"Wait. I need to grab some flowers." She hurried into the kitchen, searching for a vase large enough for the huge bunch and ending up grabbing a plastic water pitcher. In her hunt through the cupboard, something familiar caught Sierra's eye. She reached for it carefully, wrapped it in a dish towel and stuffed it in her backpack.

Tawni had her car running and was checking her

makeup in the pull-down mirror on the visor. Sierra had to brush a white paper bag off the front seat so she could sit down. A slight scent of cinnamon sugar hovered in the car. As soon as she had her seat belt on and the flowers balanced on her lap, she poked at the white bag. It was empty.

"What was in there?"

"In where?"

"The white bag. Was it a cinnamon roll from Mama Bear's?"

"Yes. What about it?" Tawni's voice still had that irritable edge to it.

"Nothing. I've been craving one of those rolls, that's all." Sierra swallowed the saliva that had filled her mouth. If she had been with anyone else, she probably would have had no qualms about slashing open the bag and licking up the crumbs. Sierra thought, *You hang on, tummy. I promise you a cinnamon roll from Mama Bear's will visit you very soon.*

Sierra led Tawni to the hospital room, where they found Granna Mae asleep in the bed and Mom dozing in the chair.

"I'll fix these," Sierra whispered, motioning with the pitcher and flowers as she stepped into the small bathroom. Mom stirred and greeted Tawni with surprise. They whispered as Sierra filled the pitcher with water. She wished she could hear what they were saying. Tawni would tell Mom what the problem was with the ski trip long before she would tell Sierra.

"Lovey?" Granna Mae called out, her voice cracked.

"I'm right here," Sierra said, going to her bedside with the pitcher of flowers. "Charlotte at the flower shop sent these for you. Aren't they beautiful?"

"Daffies," Granna Mae said with a hint of delight. "My favorite."

"I'll put them right over here," Sierra said. "Mom and Tawni are here too."

The two women came over to the bedside, and Granna Mae lifted her free arm to grasp Tawni's hand. "Nee-Nee," Granna Mae said, receiving Tawni's kiss on her cheek. Granna Mae had nicknames for all the grandchildren. Sierra just happened to be the one who was endowed with the most "normal"-sounding one. Tawni had actually acquired hers compliments of Sierra. When Sierra couldn't pronounce "Tawni" as a toddler, she called her big sister "Nee-Nee," and it had stuck for Granna Mae. Sierra's two younger brothers had both called Sierra "Sissy," but that didn't stick. Granna Mae had christened Sierra her "little lovey" from day one.

"How are you feeling?" Tawni asked.

"Okay, but not quite wonderful." Granna Mae tried to prop herself up. Tawni adjusted the pillows for her.

"You've been through a lot, Granna Mae. You don't have to feel wonderful for at least another two days." Tawni smiled and smoothed back Granna Mae's fluffy white hair. "I brought some lotion. Would you like me to rub your feet?"

"Oh, would you, Nee-Nee? They feel so cold. And could you see about possibly getting me a warm wash-cloth for my face?"

"I'll get it," Sierra volunteered, slipping back into the bathroom.

"Think you can eat a bit more of your lunch here?" Mom asked.

The three women went to work, tending their favorite patient. And Granna Mae ate it up. Sierra felt grateful for this window of time when Granna Mae was coherent. She wondered how long it would last.

"What day is this?" Granna Mae asked.

"Saturday," Mom said.

"Aren't you supposed to be at Mount Bachelor, Nee-Nee?"

"I came home early," Tawni said. "It didn't turn out to be the way I thought it would."

"Did you ski at all?" Mom asked.

"Yesterday I skied all day. The snow was a little icy, and it was too foggy for me up at the top. But it was a good day."

"So the night was the problem," Granna Mae surmised, her eyes clear and her mind obviously sharp.

Tawni looked at Mom and back at Granna Mae. She held the bottle of lotion in her hand. Before she poured any, she said, "I guess you could say that. I need to find some friends who have the same idea I do of what constitutes a fun time."

Sierra wondered if she should bring up the subject

of where they went to church. She and Tawni had talked about it with their parents before, but Mom and Dad were reluctant to approach the topic with Granna Mae. The church they all attended was Granna Mae's. It was a good church, small, traditional, and full of wonderful, sweet, elderly people with a few young families thrown in. No teenagers attended, and no youth programs or even Sunday school classes existed for them.

The family discussions had always come to the same conclusion: "We go to church as a family to worship, not to fulfill our personal social needs." Yet here they were, with Sierra and Tawni both facing the same dilemma of unmet social needs. They had tried to convince their parents that when you're sixteen and eighteen years old, spiritual needs and social needs are closely related.

"We need to find a church that has a strong youth group and college group," Sierra said as she smoothed the warm washcloth across Granna Mae's forehead. The minute she said it, she saw Mom give her a facial signal that Sierra shouldn't have spoken.

"Don't let me stop you," Granna Mae said with her eyes closed, awaiting another swipe from the washcloth.

Sierra held the cloth over Granna Mae's eyes just a moment longer than needed so she could catch Mom's expression. Tawni was looking at Mom expectantly too. Mom looked surprised. She gave her shoulders a slight shrug and nodded.

"We'll still come with you to your church some-times, Granna Mae," Sierra said, boldly plunging for-ward. "You don't mind, though, do you, if our family finds another church that sort of meets all our needs? And maybe you can visit our new church with us sometimes."

"That would be fine with me, Lovey."

Sierra ran one more wipe of the cloth over the eyes and flashed a wry smile, expecting looks of admira-tion from her mom and sister. She had just accom-plished something her dad wouldn't even try, extracting Grandma's blessing to try another church.

Mom and Tawni beamed their appreciation.

Patting Granna Mae's soft face dry with a second washcloth, Sierra said, "I brought something else for you." She reached in her backpack for the wadded-up dish towel and carefully unwrapped a china cup and saucer and held them up for Granna Mae to see. She always drank from a china cup at home. Juice, coffee, or water, whatever the liquid, a cup was always her choice. But coffee was her favorite beverage. "Shall I ring the maid to bring you some hot coffee?"

chapter nine

"I THINK WE SHOULD TRY THE ONE IN VANCOUVER," Tawni said. She was stretched out comfortably on her bed that night while Sierra was making an honest attempt to pick up her clothes. Mom sat on the corner of Sierra's unmade bed.

"It's so far away," Mom said. "That's been the benefit of Granna Mae's church. It's only three blocks from here. Besides, it seems odd to go to a church in another state."

"But Washington is only across the river. It wouldn't take more than fifteen minutes to drive there. And I've heard that this church in Vancouver has the best college group around," Tawni said.

"I've heard something at school about a church out in Gresham that's pretty good," Sierra added.

"Gresham is at least a twenty-minute drive in the opposite direction," Mom protested.

"See? We're better off going to Vancouver. I already called. The service is at ten tomorrow morning." Tawni put on her ridiculous-looking glasses she wore only to read and opened up her paperback book.

"I wish your father was home so we could all discuss this. Maybe we should go to Granna Mae's church one last time tomorrow morning, and then next week we can start to visit other churches."

"Why?" Sierra asked.

"What would be the point of that?" Tawni chimed in. "Granna Mae won't be there. This is the best time to make a change."

Mom let out a sigh and held up her hands in surrender. "I'm too tired to argue. You two make the decision. I'll go wherever you choose. Right now I'm going to bed. Has anyone checked the answering machine?"

"Nope."

"I'm concerned about Gayle. She wasn't doing too well when I left, and I'm afraid Darren isn't much help."

"Why is he so uptight all the time?" Sierra asked. "I thought he was going to bite my head off on the phone yesterday."

Mom sighed again. She hesitated before saying, "Their marriage is in a difficult place right now. He was laid off last month, and the insurance might not cover Gayle's hospitalization. You know what a handful the twins are. It's rough for them."

"Do you wish you would have stayed with them?" Sierra asked. "We could have taken care of Granna Mae."

Mom shook her head. "Darren's sister was coming

in this evening. She'll do a better job than I did with Darren and the twins. If you two have never thought about thanking God for the father He gave you ..."

"You mean instead of someone like Darren?" Sierra asked.

"I'm just saying, be thankful for the daddy you got. I sometimes forget what a wonderful husband and father Howard is." Mom rose to leave and then stopped. "You know what? Let's pray together before I go to bed. Just like when you two were little."

Sierra followed Mom over to Tawni's bed, where the three women sat cross-legged in a circle and joined hands. They prayed for Granna Mae, for Dad and the boys, and for Aunt Gayle and Uncle Darren. Mom choked up as she was praying for Gayle and Darren, and Sierra felt a knot tighten in the pit of her stomach as Mom asked God to rescue their marriage and protect the twins.

Then Mom did something very tender. She prayed for Tawni's and Sierra's future husbands. She prayed that they would surrender their lives to the Lord, if they hadn't already, and that they would be set apart as godly men who would one day love Tawni and Sierra and their children. As Mom prayed, she wept.

Sierra felt the tears well up in her own eyes as she silently agreed with her mother's prayer. She knew her mother had prayed this for her many times, just as Granna Mae had once prayed for the spouses of her eleven children. Sierra's mom had been the answer to

Granna Mae's long years of prayers for Howard. All her life Sierra's parents and Granna Mae had prayed for Sierra and for her future husband. She had become used to it.

Until tonight. Tonight her mother's prayers sounded fresh and powerful in Sierra's ears. In her heart, she realized she was holding hands with a mighty warrior. Supernatural events were being released on her behalf because of her mother's prayers to Almighty God.

Mom closed her prayer with "In the name of Jesus, may it be so."

Sierra looked up through teary eyes. "May it be so," she repeated.

"Amen," Tawni echoed.

"I love you two," Mom said, giving them each a hug and a kiss on the cheek.

"I love you too, Mom." Sierra brushed a kiss across Mom's cheek. "And I even love you," she said to Tawni with a smile and a lightening of her serious tone. Tawni accepted Sierra's peck on the cheek but didn't respond in kind.

"Sleep well," Mom said with a yawn. "Wake me if I'm not up by nine."

"We're going to Vancouver, then?" Tawni asked.

"Fine with me," Sierra said.

"Sure," Mom said, as she yawned again and stumbled out the door.

Sierra shoved her stuff off the bed and crawled under her covers. She could feel Tawni's critical glare.

"What?" she asked without looking at her sister.

"Aren't you going to finish picking up your junk?"

"Tomorrow. I'll do it tomorrow," Sierra said in her best Scarlett O'Hara voice.

"Tomorrow" turned into several tomorrows. Finally, on Tuesday Sierra attacked the mound of clothes again. This time she was determined to clean up everything. Or, at least Tawni was determined that Sierra change the landscape of their room.

They had gotten along pretty well the last few days. They both had liked the church in Vancouver, and Tawni actually had let Sierra borrow her precious car Monday afternoon to visit Granna Mae in the hospital while Tawni dressed for work.

Granna Mae was improving nicely, and the doctor had said she could go home Saturday, if all went well the rest of the week. She slept most of the time, but her memory had been good when she was awake.

Sierra sorted out the dirty clothes from the clean. Then she scooped up the dirty clothes and headed for the washing machine in the basement. She had just put her first load in when she heard her dad's voice upstairs. Dad had spent most of his free time at the hospital since he had returned from camping. Gavin and Dillon had quickly filled the house with lots of noise again. Everything seemed back to normal.

But not quite. While the crisis had passed for Granna Mae, Sierra's problems remained unsolved. She still didn't have a job. She still didn't have a social life. And she desperately wanted to go to Southern California during Easter vacation. For that she would need her dad's approval. And now that Dad had settled back into a routine, it was time to ask.

Sierra took the basement steps two at a time. She found her father in the kitchen, washing off an apple before taking a big chomp out of it.

"Oh, Daddy, my wonderful Daddy-o!" Sierra began, looping her arm around his shoulders.

"How much is it going to cost me?" Dad asked without blinking.

Sierra drew back her arm. "What makes you think I'm going to ask for money?"

"You are, aren't you?"

"Well, not exactly."

"But whatever it is you're going to ask, it's going to cost money, right?"

Sierra circled her arm around him again and playfully rested her head on his shoulder. "How did you ever get to be so wise and wonderful, oh, Daddy, my wonderful Daddy-o?"

He looked down at her, and she batted her eyelashes for emphasis. Howard Jensen broke out laughing and nearly choked on his bite of apple. "Looks like this is serious," he said, still laughing. "Better step into my office."

"Dad!" Gavin called from the backyard in his high-pitched, six-year-old voice. "Can you come out and help us?"

"What do you need, son?"

"The pulley on the tree-house rope broke."

"I'll be out in about . . . , " Dad looked at Sierra. "What do you think?" he asked her. "Twenty minutes? Half an hour? Three hours?"

"Twenty minutes," Sierra said. "It's a simple request, really."

"I'll be out in twenty minutes," Dad called back. "Don't try to fix it without me, okay, guys?"

"We won't," Dillon, the ever-clever eight-year-old, called back.

"Yeah, right," Dad muttered under his breath. He took another bite out of his apple. "Right this way," he said, leading Sierra into the office.

This was Dad's favorite room in the house, and it was becoming Sierra's favorite hideaway too. One whole wall was a floor-to-ceiling bookshelf. Several rows were stacked with old books from Granna Mae's lifelong collection. Many were in Danish, her original language. The books had an intriguing, musty smell that made the room feel important and familiar at the same time. It was a room full of silent friends who stood ever ready to give, yet who demanded nothing in return except perhaps an occasional dusting.

Sierra's favorite chair was nestled in the corner next to the French doors that opened to the back patio. When the sun shone in, it hit that chair just right. Any cat would love to claim the seat as its own private tanning booth. No sun was beaming through the windows today, but that didn't stop Sierra from settling into the chair and stretching out her legs so her feet rested on the matching, stuffed footstool.

Dad took a seat in the revolving oak captain's chair by the rolltop desk and leaned back. "Okay, shoot," he said, chomping into his afternoon snack.

"I want to go see the friends I met in England. They've invited me for Easter vacation. I'd fly down to San Diego or Orange County airport, and I'll pay for the whole thing myself. It's just that I don't have any money. Zilch."

"Oh," Dad said calmly, "is that all?"

"I tried to get a job at the flower shop, but they wanted me to work Sundays and use my own car. I haven't tried anywhere else, but I want to get a job around here so I can walk and not have to depend on the car."

"Sounds wise," Dad said.

"So, may I go?"

"I'll talk with your mother about it. I'm sure it'll be fine for you to go for the week, but you're right. You'll need to pay for the airfare. This recent quick trip to Phoenix for your mom wasn't exactly in the budget. I'll tell you what. Why don't you work on finding a job, and I'll work on finding the lowest airfare. Does it matter which airport? Your friends are going to pick you up, aren't they?"

"Of course. I don't think it matters. They live kind of between both airports."

"Okay," Dad said. "I'll check out the airfares."

Sierra flashed a big smile. "Thank you, my wonderful Daddy-o!"

"Don't get too confident now, Sierra. It's still contingent on you coming up with the airfare."

"I know. But thanks for just being my dad."

"Any time," Dad said, opening the French doors and heading toward the tree house. "By the way," he called over his shoulder, "did you see the mail on the desk? There's a letter for you."

chapter ten

SIERRA SPRANG FROM HER COZY CHAIR AND GRABBED
the stack of letters on top of the desk. Bills, bills,
advertisement. Her hand stopped on a white
envelope addressed to Sierra Jensen in bold black letters. She immediately recognized the handwriting. She
had only received one other letter with that script, but
she had read it at least fifty times. Maybe more. Right
this minute, that letter with the matching handwriting
was under her pillow. And today, its twin had come.

Cradling the letter in her hands, Sierra returned
to her nesting chair and turned the envelope over and
over before she opened it. *Did Paul write it before he
saw me on Saturday or after? What if he's writing just to
make fun of me?*

Unable to stand it another second, Sierra carefully
opened the envelope and lifted out the one sheet of
white writing paper. Only a few lines in Paul's distinctive handwriting, which was a combination of cursive and printing in bold, black letters, appeared on
the page. It said:

Dear Daffodil Queen,
    I was wondering, and of course it's none of
my business, but just out of curiosity, do you
have pneumonia yet? And if you do, should I
send flowers? Or will your lovely bouquet last
you the duration of your convalescence?

Sincerely,
A Casual Observer

Sierra read the letter four times, deciphering it dif-
ferently each time. At first it was funny. Then it was
sort of sweet. The third time it seemed pretty rude to
her. By the fourth reading, she was mad.
    Marching over to the desk, Sierra found a piece
of lined notebook paper and started to write before
she had a chance to change her mind:

    For your information, Mr. Hotshot, my
grandmother is in the hospital. I was the only
one home with her Friday morning when we
received the call that she needed emergency
surgery. I stayed up with her all night in the
hospital room. When you saw me, I was walking
home from a job interview with daffodils that
had been given to me to take to my Granna Mae
because those happen to be her favorite flower.
    To answer your questions:
    Yes, it's none of your business.

No, I don't have pneumonia.

No, I don't want any stupid flowers from you. I already told you the flowers were for my grandmother, who, by the way, is still in the hospital.

And, in case you're wondering, no, I didn't get the job.

Oh, and don't go around signing things "sincerely" unless you really are.

Very Irritatedly,
Sierra

Then, before she had a chance to change her mind, Sierra folded the paper, tucked it in an envelope, and fished around in the top drawer for a stamp. She hoofed it up to her room and snatched the previous letter from underneath her pillow. She looked at it just long enough to obtain the necessary post office box number and then wadded up the precious letter and tossed it at the wicker trash can. She missed. The letter landed near a stack of school papers.

Sierra galloped down the stairs and called out to her dad in the backyard. "I'm going to mail a letter, Dad."

"Hang on, Sierra," he called back from his workshop. It was an old playhouse he had turned into a shop. Inside it was all power tools, but the outside looked as if Hansel and Gretel might stop by at any moment. Dad opened the Dutch door, wiping his hand on a towel. He reached in his pocket and pulled out some money. "Can you swing by Mama Bear's and pick up a box of cinnamon rolls? I told Granna Mae I'd bring her breakfast tomorrow morning."

"You don't know how much I'd love to do that for you, Dad," Sierra said. "And I don't need any money."

"I thought you were broke. Zilch."

"Mom told me to take some out of the desk when she was gone. I've been using it for lunch money and gas money. I have enough left for a box of cinnamon rolls."

Dad grinned and said, "I guess I'll have to find another hiding place for my loot."

"Come on, Dad," Gavin called from the tree house.

"Do you want to take my car?" Dad asked.

"No, I need the exercise. I'll be right back." Sierra took off with long strides, clutching the letter in her hand the four blocks to the mailbox. It was a good thing the box wasn't farther away or the sweat on her palms might have soaked through the envelope. With a yank on the handle, she shoved the letter into the dark abyss.

Instantly she regretted it. Sierra stood there, glancing around to see if anyone was watching her. She wondered if she could somehow retrieve her letter. It soon became obvious she couldn't. What was done was done.

She realized she needed the consolation of a cinnamon roll from Mama Bear's. She covered the next seven or so blocks at a near-jogging pace. The moment she entered the shop, she felt relieved, as if she had run a race against her hurt and anger and had beat them.

The store was empty except for three people who were huddling over fragrant coffee in the middle of some sort of meeting at one of the side tables. The scent of cinnamon wasn't as strong as it had been on Saturday morning, but it was still there, permeating the room.

"Are you still open?" Sierra asked the round woman in the white ruffly apron who was wiping down the counter.

"Another five minutes," the rosy cheeked woman said, glancing at the clock that broadcast the time as "5:55." It was a wooden clock in the shape of a brown bear. Its big, round tummy was the clock's face.

"Good! I'm glad I made it," Sierra said. "I need a box of rolls."

The woman reached over to the rack behind her and grabbed a box. "Can I get you anything else?"

Whenever a waitress would ask that question, Sierra's brother Cody would always answer, "Yeah, a couple of tickets to Maui. To go, please." Sierra smiled and answered, "A ticket to San Diego."

The woman looked confused for just a moment, but then she smiled. "Getting a little tired of the rain, are you? Anxious to see some sunshine?"

Sierra nodded. "Actually, I'm hoping to visit some friends down there during Easter vacation. All I need is the money to buy my airplane ticket. But first I need a job to earn the money to buy the ticket." Sierra realized she was pouring out her heart to a stranger and quickly said, "But for today, all I need is a box of your world-famous cinnamon rolls. I've been craving them for days!"

The woman took the money Sierra held out to her and rang up the purchase on the cash register. "You're not going to eat this whole box by yourself, are you?"

"I'll try not to." Sierra smiled as the white-aproned Mama Bear tucked the box into a large, white paper bag. "I need to save at least one of these for my Granna Mae, who's waiting for it in the hospital."

"You don't mean Mae Jensen, do you?"

"Yes, she's my grandmother."

"Well, I'll be! And which one are you?"

"Sierra."

"And your parents are . . . "

"Howard and Sharon."

"No!" the sweet woman said, clasping her hands around her middle like an opera singer. "My brother went to school with Howard. I used to have such a crush on him! Tell him you saw Amelia. Amelia Kraus now, but I was Amelia Jackson. And tell him to come in sometime."

"I know he's been here before," Sierra said.

"I don't usually work at the counter. My husband and I own this shop. But it's been so busy lately, I've had to put the apron back on. And your grandmother? Is she okay?"

"She had her gall bladder out. She's doing fine."

"Goodness gracious! You be sure and tell Howard hello for us and get him in here sometime."

"I will," Sierra said, tucking the bag in the crook of her arm. "Thanks again! It was very nice meeting you."

"You too, Sierra," Mrs. Kraus said, following her to the door, where she turned over the "open" sign. "Bye now."

Sierra stepped out into the chilly street, where the smell of wet sidewalks and car exhaust instantly assaulted her. They were a rude contrast to the warm cinnamon and coffee smells of Mama Bear's. She took about four steps when she was overpowered by the obvious. Turning around, she walked two steps before the door of Mama Bear's opened again, and Mrs. Kraus popped out her head. Both of them spoke at the same time, and then they both laughed.

"You first," Sierra said.

"It just occurred to me, you said you were looking for a job, and—"

"I had the same thought," Sierra said.

"Well, then come back in, my dear," she said, opening the door wide. "I believe Providence has designed this moment."

chapter eleven

"I'M HOME!" SIERRA CALLED OUT, AS THE FRONT door slammed behind her.

"We're in here," Mom called from the dining room.

Sierra shelved the cinnamon rolls in the pantry and found her family seated around the antique dining room table eating Mom's favorite "speedy dinner"—baked potatoes with steamed broccoli and cheese.

"Guess what?" Sierra said breathlessly.

Everyone looked at her expectantly.

"You ran into an Elvis impersonator from Mars who eats human brains," Dillon said.

"Yeah," Gavin added, "and he tried to suck your brain, but he starved."

"Boys," Dad said firmly. "What's the news, Sierra?"

Not even her brothers' dumb jokes could dampen her enthusiasm. "I got a job! At Mama Bear's. I start Thursday. My hours are four to six on Tuesdays and Thursdays, and eight to four Saturdays. It's perfect! And Mrs. Kraus knows you, Dad. Her name was

Amelia Jackson before she got married, and she said you should come in sometime. *And* she gave us an extra box of cinnamon rolls free. But the best part is, she already said I could have the time off during Easter vacation!" Sierra paused just long enough to catch her breath. "And she's a Christian. Can you believe that? Did you know they don't open their shop on Sundays? Is that incredible or what?"

"It's incredible," Mom agreed.

"Mrs. Kraus called it 'Providence.' Something about God's leading in ways we can't see or understand." Sierra speared a potato from the serving bowl and poked it open with her fork, allowing the steam to escape.

"Our God is an awesome God," Dad said. It was his favorite saying, and he often sang a chorus with the same words. "I guess I better start to check on those airline tickets."

"Where's she going?" Dillon asked.

"Please don't talk when your mouth is full, Dillon. Sierra wants to go down to Southern California during Easter to visit her friends," Mom explained.

"So it's okay with you, Mom?" Sierra found it impossible to suppress her excitement.

"With the conditions as Dad explained, sure."

Tawni, who hadn't said anything yet, dropped her fork onto her plate and said, "Does anyone else have a problem with her getting to fly off to England *and* California while the rest of us stay home?"

"We went camping," Gavin said.

"Yeah, and you went skiing," Dillon said. "And Sierra was the only one home that time."

Tawni rolled her eyes. "That ski trip was a disaster!"

"You can come to San Diego with me if you want," Sierra blurted out.

"Oh, right! And what would I do there? Hang out with you and all your little friends?"

"They're not 'little friends,'" Sierra said. "I'm the youngest of all of them. Katie and Christy are your age; Tracy, Doug, and Todd are all in their twenties."

Tawni gave Sierra a strange look as if this was new information to her. "And what are they doing inviting you down there?"

"They're my friends. They treat me as an equal." Sierra's exuberance began to dwindle as she defended herself to her sister. She *did* see herself on the same level with Katie, Christy, and the others. With Tawni, she always felt inferior.

"Congratulations on the job," Mom said, redirecting the conversation. "I'm sure that will be a fun place to work."

"I couldn't do it," Tawni said, excusing herself from the table and clearing her plate. "I'd gain twenty pounds a day just smelling those rolls. Too bad the flower shop didn't work out. Much less fattening."

Sierra had never been seriously concerned about her weight. She had her mom's quick metabolism and had always been active enough to burn off excess sweets. Tawni was the relentless calorie counter in the family. She was adopted and more than once expressed her fear that her biological mother might be a blimp.

"Do we get to have cinnamon rolls for dessert?" Dillon asked. He was an eight-year-old version of their dad and had inherited his sweet tooth.

"Let's wait till breakfast," Mom said. "Is anyone planning to see Granna Mae tonight?"

"I can go over," Dad said. "Do you boys want to go with me?"

"Whose turn is it to help with the dishes?" Mom asked.

"Sierra's," Gavin said.

"Naturally," Sierra muttered, rising to clear the dishes. The first handful of plates clattered as they came to rest in the stainless steel sink.

"Take it easy in there," Mom called out.

"I am," Sierra said. She didn't know why she hated doing the dishes so much. Rinsing them off and loading them into the dishwasher certainly wasn't hard. Mom always worked alongside her, and they usually had good talks. But something happened inside Sierra every time she was told that it was her turn to do the dishes. It was like a mean button was pushed inside her. And if she opened the dishwasher and found it full of clean dishes that hadn't been put away yet, the "mean-o-meter" automatically turned up about three notches. She knew it was dumb. Still, there it was. Tonight her fully operative mean-o-meter quickly rose as she opened the dishwasher and found it full of clean dishes.

The chore only took fifteen minutes or so, and as always, Mom thanked her for helping. Sierra mumbled, "You're welcome," and excused herself to do her homework.

When she reached her room, Tawni was already at the desk working on her homework from one of the courses she was taking at the community college. Without a word, Sierra cleared a spot on her bed and started to read her very boring government textbook.

The two sisters worked in silence for more than an hour before Tawni said, "Were you serious about my going to San Diego with you?"

Sierra hesitated. She had extended the invitation in a jovial moment. In truth, the last person she wanted to spend Easter with was Tawni. And never, in her right mind, would she have thought to let Tawni loose on her circle of sacred friends. One look at the perfect Tawni and Sierra would be an instant castoff. "Why do you ask?" Sierra said cautiously.

Tawni turned to Sierra. Tears were in her eyes. "I just wanted to know if you really meant it."

"Sure," Sierra said, instantly motivated by the uncommon display of emotion. She knew Tawni was trying to make friends too. That need was about the only thing they shared right now.

Tawni didn't respond. She turned back around and bent over her books.

"So?" Sierra prodded. "What are you saying? Do you want to come with me or what?"

"I'm not sure," Tawni said in a low voice. "I'll let you know."

Sierra felt like throwing a pillow at her sister. It was bad enough that Sierra had made the crazy invitation. Tawni could at least say yes or no so Sierra would know whether or not her life was about to be ruined. This limbo game was *not* to Sierra's liking. But it was typical of Tawni to keep others waiting on her.

Whenever Sierra felt this frustrated and angry, she knew the best thing, the only thing, that helped was to get her face into her Bible and leave it there until she had an answer. She reached for the leather-covered treasure on her nightstand and opened to where a crinkled candy bar wrapper marked her place. She began to read where she had left off a few days ago.

Sierra's method of devotions was to read through a whole book at a time. Some days she would read only a few verses, but other days it would be several chapters. Whenever she missed a day, instead of feeling guilty, Sierra would just pick up where she had left off. She also kept a notebook in which she logged thoughts that came to her as she read.

The marker was in the twenty-sixth chapter of Isaiah. She had been reading in Isaiah for more than a week and admittedly had skimmed some of the earlier chapters. The last few had been more interesting to her, and she had underlined some passages.

Tonight she read slowly and stopped at verse three. "You will keep him in perfect peace, whose mind is stayed on You, because he trusts in You."

Sierra turned her back to her sister and read the verse again. She wondered how much she trusted God and how much she depended on herself to make things happen in her life. She read on. The next phrase that stopped her was in verse nine: "With my soul I have desired You in the night."

I don't know if I desire You like that, God. I want to. I want to trust You every day for everything. I also want to . . . She read the phrase again. . . . *I want my soul to desire You, Father God. I want You in my whole life. Not just in my crazy days. I want You in my restless nights. I want You in my dreams.*

Instead of feeling stronger and peaceful and more spiritual, Sierra felt bummed out. Not so much about Tawni. Tawni was her ongoing unsettled relationship. What Sierra felt yucky about tonight was the letter she had sent to Paul. Her words had been an impulsive reaction that showed her sassy side and would surely sever any potential relationship that might have been developed with Paul. And it was too late to do anything about it.

chapter twelve

SIERRA REACHED INTO THE BAG AND PULLED OUT another Sun Chip. French onion. Her favorite. In the other hand she held a copy of the school newspaper. She was scanning the back page, reading the classifieds and contemplating the notice in the lower righthand corner. "All personals and ads must be submitted by Friday at noon. Please bring them to the journalism office along with exact payment at two cents a word."

Filtering out the lunchroom noise around her, Sierra pulled out a piece of paper and fiddled with a few words. She had thought Katie's idea of advertising for a friend was silly at the time, but today, as she sat alone again at the indoor lunch table, the idea seemed to have some merit.

"Wanted," she scribbled. "Someone to eat lunch with." She crossed it out and tried again. "Looking for a pal? I've been looking for you." She skipped down a few lines and tried, "New girl in school seeking a way to break into one of your extremely tight cliques. Please advise."

"That's easy," a male voice behind her said. Sierra snatched up her scratch paper and spun around to give whomever it was a dirty look.

"Whoa!" he said. "My advice is to lighten up." It was Randy, the first student she had met at Royal Academy. He had shown her around the first day and more than once had tried to start up conversations with her. Sierra had usually answered with one-syllable responses, shrugged her shoulders, and pulled away. Even though she had made a few tries here and there to talk to people in her classes, more often she had drawn back and kept to herself.

Sierra suddenly realized how she must look to the other students. It was as if her mean-o-meter, which clicked on every time she had to do the dishes, had also become fully activated at school. She had not made much effort to break into any of the circles of friends.

Randy sat down next to Sierra even though he hadn't been invited. He gave his head a shake and a tilt, flipping back his straight blond hair. "You know what, Sierra Jensen? It's time we had a talk."

"Oh, really?" she said, her tone teasing.

"Really," Randy said. "It's time for you to get a life."

She felt a twinge of anger surfacing.

Randy must have read it in her face because he leaned closer and broke into his crooked grin. Sierra noticed the stubble of a faint beard shading his jaw line. "May I start over?" Randy asked.

Sierra nodded.

"Will you be my friend?" His clear eyes reflected his sincerity.

"Why? You already have plenty of friends."

"See?" Randy slapped his hand on the table for emphasis. "That is the problem! Why won't you let anyone in? Why are you so guarded all the time?"

"I don't know," Sierra said honestly. She felt unwanted tears building up in her eyes and quickly blinked and swallowed so they wouldn't break free.

Randy kept looking at her; his open expression didn't change. The bell rang right over their heads, and the lunchroom began to clear out, but Randy didn't move. He sat there, looking at Sierra, waiting. She glanced away, feeling uncomfortable. Part of her wanted to open up to him and tell him that she didn't feel accepted here, that she felt like an outsider. But deep down she knew that 90 percent of that was her fault. Maybe even more. She had withdrawn big-time.

The odd part was that such behavior was the opposite of her personality. Up until this point in her life she had always been the initiator. She had been the "Randy" at school and church, trying to make everyone else feel welcome. Now she was the new girl, and she didn't know how to play the role.

"Well, when you decide you're ready to conduct interviews for a buddy, I'd like to apply for the job."

Sierra let her smile surface. She felt foolish and immature for being unwilling to talk with him.

"Randy," she began, "it's hard—"

"No, it isn't," he said. "You haven't tried yet."

Sierra wished she had some magic words to make everything better. Words that she could use like a ticket to allow her to try this ride again.

Then she remembered something one of the speakers had said on her missions trip in England. She had written it in her notebook and had noticed it a few nights ago. He had said, "When all is said and done, there will only be two phrases to sum up every relationship. The first is 'Forgive me.' The second is 'Thank you.' Say the first often in your youth, and you will need only the second on your deathbed."

"Randy," Sierra said quickly, "forgive me."

"Okay. But what am I forgiving you for?"

"For being a brat. I would rather be your buddy."

Randy tossed her one of his crooked smiles. "You mean I got the job?"

"Yup." She stood up and held out her hand to shake on it. "You're hired."

Instead of a handshake, Randy looped his arm around her shoulders and gave Sierra a sideways hug.

"Pals?" Randy asked.

Sierra remembered the Pals Only Club she and Katie had joked about. "Pals," she echoed.

"Come on," he said. "We're going to be late."

Sierra grabbed her backpack and tossed her crumpled-up ad for a new friend into the trash can on their way out the door. For the first time, she had someone to walk with her to class.

After school, Randy and two other girls, Amy and Vicki, stopped her before she reached her car in the parking lot. Sierra had talked some with the girls before, and they had both tried to pursue a friendship with Sierra, but she hadn't done much to reciprocate.

Amy looked Italian with thick, black hair and dark, expressive eyes. More than once she had come to school wearing an outfit similar to one of Sierra's.

Vicki was very popular. Her stunning looks had something to do with that. She wore her silky brown hair parted down the middle, and it billowed at her shoulders in a slight wave. Her almond-shaped, green eyes were arched by thin eyebrows, and she had a rather "womanly" figure. Because Vicki was so attractive, Sierra had assumed she was stuck up and hadn't thought much about talking with her before.

The three friends gathered around Sierra and said, "We're going to McDonald's. You want to come?"

"I have to work," Sierra said. "Today's my first day. I have to be there by four."

"Where do you work?" Vicki asked.

"It's a little shop on Hawthorne that makes cinnamon rolls."

"Mama Bear's?" Amy said. "I love that place. You know where it is, Vicki. On the same side of the street as my favorite dress shop, A Wrinkle in Time."

"Oh, yeah," Vicki said. "Maybe we should go there instead of McDonald's."

Sierra swallowed hard. This making new friends

thing was pretty awkward for her. Starting a brand-new job would probably be uncomfortable too, but combining both activities sounded like a disaster. She felt relieved when Randy said, "They don't have burgers there, do they? I'm in search of some real food."

"Aw, come on, Randy," Amy said. "They have lattés."

Apparently the lure of fancy coffee drinks wasn't enough to coerce Randy to change his mind. "How about another time?" he suggested.

"Sounds good to me." Sierra let out her breath, which she realized she had been holding.

"We'll see you tomorrow," Vicki said.

They turned to go. Sierra unlocked the car door and then stopped and called out, "Hey!" They turned around. "Thank you," she said.

"Sure," Randy answered for the three of them. He didn't seem quite clear on what she was thanking them for.

Sierra felt good as she drove to Mama Bear's. She was making progress. This wasn't a result of chance. When peace came blowing in like this, riding on the wind of the Holy Spirit, God was at work.

She rolled down the window, stuck out her elbow into the cool afternoon air, and peeked through the windshield into the cloudy sky. "Thank You," she whispered.

Well, now you know. I tried to wash some of it in the sink at work, but it was impossible. I can't [be]lieve they didn't throw me out and threaten my life [if] I ever darkened their doorway again. Oh, and then [the] grand finale. Right before it was time for me to leave, I caught my apron on the edge of this big mixer they have in the back, and I tore the apron."

"A lot?" Mom asked.

Sierra held up her two index fingers in the air to indicate a rip of about seven inches.

Mom covered her mouth. Sierra knew her mother was trying hard to suppress her laughter.

"And they still want you to come back on Saturday?" Dad asked.

"Yes. Absolutely amazing, isn't it?"

"By any chance did the job description call for someone to provide comic relief?" Dad teased. "You know, perk up the business a little by putting on a sideshow. Customers will be lining up on the days you work just to see what's going to happen next."

Sierra grabbed a pot holder off the counter next to her and threw it at her dad. "You meanie!"

"Meanie?" Dad said, catching the pot holder before it hit Mom. "What happened to 'wonderful Daddy-o' who was checking on airline tickets for you?"

"What did you find out?" Sierra said, ducking as the pot holder came flying back at her.

"What's for dinner, honey?"

"Chicken soup. It's ready."

chapter thirteen

"SIERRA, IS THAT YOU?" MOM CALLED FROM THE kitchen.

"Yes, it's your very own walking disaster." Sierra dragged herself into the kitchen, dropped into a chair, pulled back her hair, and held it on top of her head in a ponytail. "You will not believe what happened."

Mom turned down the flame on a big pot of soup and said, "Oh, I might. Give me a try."

Sierra let down her hair and started her story. "I got to Mama Bear's on time. A little early, actually. They had this nice blue apron waiting for me, and Mrs. Kraus started to show me how to make cappuccinos. Should be simple, right?" Sierra shook her head. "I go to make my first one for this guy who's standing right there watching me, but I didn't tighten the little filter thing enough. You know, that thing with the handle that you use to put the coffee grounds in and clamp it onto the part where the super-hot water comes out."

"Don't tell me," Mom said.

"I did. I turned on the machine, and it spit scald-
ing water all over my pretty new apron, all over the
floor, and all over the counter. When I tried to stop it,
it spewed soggy coffee grounds all over. And I do mean
all over. It was a disaster."

"That's awful, honey!"

"Wait. There's more. Mrs. Kraus is nice, calm, and
sweet, and she tells me to start over and not to worry
about it. So I clean up everything, and I try again, very
carefully. Everything is perfect. The steamed milk
frothed up just right. Wonderful. Only one problem.
I forgot to put any coffee grounds in. I can't believe
it! I was so worried about the machine that I wasn't
paying attention to the cup. Then I hand this guy his
cappuccino after he's been waiting for ten minutes.
He takes one sip and practically sprays it out of his
mouth and all over the counter."

"Oh, Sierra," Mom sympathized.

"He gets really mad, and in front of about ten
customers, he demands his money back and says he's
never coming back. I thought he was going to throw
the cup at me. I thought Mrs. Kraus was going to fire
me right then and there."

"Did she?"

"No. She was totally calm and said, 'These things
happen. Try again.'"

"What a marvelous attitude."

"I know. She's a very sweet woman."

"And did you try again?"

"Yes. I got it right
cappuccino for the very ne
at me the whole time, which
Then when I handed the cup t
dollar tip and said, 'I think all ch
rewarded.'"

Mom smiled and shook her head. "C
And all this on your first day!"

"That's not all," Sierra said.

"You're kidding!"

Dad had entered the kitchen with Brutus's
leash in his hand. As he hung it on the hook on th
back door, he asked, "Is this the recap of day one at
the bakery? What have I missed so far?"

"I'll fill you in later," Mom said. "Just listen. She's
on a roll."

Sierra started to laugh. She laughed until little tear
crystals shimmered in her eyes. "Actually," she said,
"the roll was on me."

"This ought to be good," Dad said, resting his arm
on Mom's shoulder and giving Sierra his full attention.

"I reached for a box of a half-dozen cinnamon
rolls that was on this rack behind the cash register. I
didn't know, of course, that the box was open. I wasn't
paying attention, and the whole thing tumbled onto
me." She held up the ends of her hair. "Frosting everywhere."

"I wondered what happened to your hair," Mom
said. "But frankly, I wasn't sure I wanted to know."

"Dad!" Sierra pleaded.

"Chicken soup?" he said, lifting the lid and giving it a stir. "Who's sick?"

"You're going to be if you don't tell me about the airplane tickets!" Sierra jumped up and grabbed his arm before he could reach for another pot holder.

"Oh, getting tricky in your old age, are you?" Dad leaned over and took a whiff of Sierra's hair. "I like your new perfume. It has that fresh-from-the-oven fragrance. Subtle yet tasty."

"You're going to be fresh from the oven if you don't tell me about the tickets!"

"Okay, okay!" Dad said, raising both hands in surrender. Some numbers were written in blue ink on the palm of his right hand.

"What's this?" Sierra said, grabbing his hand and taking a closer look.

"I didn't have a piece of paper handy. I was on hold for so long with the remote phone that when they finally came back on the line ..."

Mom shook her head at her husband's antics.

"That one in the middle," he said pointing, "is the fare into John Wayne. It's the best price."

"John Wayne?"

"That's what they call the Orange County airport. Do you think you can come up with the money in less than three weeks?"

"I think so," Sierra said, twisting her head to read the last two numbers. "Is that a two or a five?"

"Five. I think. Let me see. Yeah, that's a five."

"When do I leave, and when do I come back?"

"You would leave on Friday evening and return the following Thursday. No seats were left for a return on the weekend, and they only had a few seats left on Thursday at this reduced price."

"You asked them to hold it for me, didn't you?"

Just then the phone rang and Mom reached for the extension on the wall.

"I most certainly did. What kind of a secretary would I be if I didn't make a reservation for my boss?"

"Oh, dear," Mom said.

Sierra and Dad stopped their teasing and turned their attention to Mom.

"Yes ... I see. ... Thank you for calling right away. Good-bye." She hung up. Her face was creased with worry lines. "We need to go right now," she said.

"Was it the hospital? Were they calling about Granna Mae?" Sierra asked.

Mom nodded. "Sierra, can you serve dinner to the boys? They both need baths, and they need to be in bed by eight. Tawni should be home from work around 9:30. Call us at the hospital if you need anything."

"Is she okay?" Sierra asked.

"I'm not sure. Howard, are you ready to go?"

"Right with you, sweetheart. Let's take the van. I have the keys."

With a whoosh, they were out the door. The

kitchen, which had rung with laughter only moments before, had turned painfully still. Sierra forced herself to take a deep breath. "Gavin! Dillon!" She called out the back door. "Time to eat."

chapter fourteen

SIERRA STEPPED OUT OF THE BATHROOM WITH A
towel wrapped around her head. She fought
the urge, which had been nagging her for the
last two and a half hours, to call the hospital. The boys
were fed, bathed, and in bed. She had solemnly loaded
the dishwasher and cleaned up the kitchen. Tawni
should be home soon. And Sierra really needed to start
working on her paper for English. It was due tomorrow, and procrastinator that she was, she hadn't begun
the five-page report.

Fortunately for Sierra, she managed to come out
of such situations unscathed. Her teachers wrote on
her report card in the comment column, "Sierra is
bright and intelligent. She has not yet pushed herself
to her full potential." It was true. She had never been
motivated to try harder. Why should she when, with
a minimum of effort, she could meet the class require-
ments and come home with a sterling report card?

She slipped into her favorite big T-shirt pajamas
and searched under her bed for her other fuzzy slipper.

Not there. She tried the closet. Nope. Sierra glanced around the room, looking for the missing slipper. Then, as if she truly noticed her side of the room for the first time, she said aloud, "What a slob! No wonder you can't find anything, girl."

That did it. She couldn't stand the mess another minute. In a frenzy of motion, Sierra kicked into high gear and started to clean her room. It didn't matter that it was after nine and she still had a paper to do. She could not stand to live in this messy room another second. She was actually feeling sympathetic for Tawni, who had to look at her disastrous mess every day.

Panting hard, her wet hair dripping down her back and wearing only one slipper, Sierra worked with lightning speed to hang up clothes, throw away papers, stuff necessary junk into drawers, and clean off the top of her dresser. She even stripped her bedsheets and jogged to the hall closet for clean, neatly folded sheets that smelled like lemon fabric softener. With a few quick folds and a snap of her comforter, Sierra's bed was made—probably for the first time since they had moved here.

Then, scooping up an armful of dirty clothes, she trucked down to the washer in the basement and started up a load. Her clothes from a few days earlier were all folded and waiting for her in a plastic laundry bucket. On top of the clothes was the missing slipper—a clean, fresh contrast to the one on her foot. In the slipper was a little note in Mom's handwriting. "Some bunny wuvs you!"

I wonder if I'll be such a terrific mom someday,
Sierra thought, lugging the clean clothes upstairs. Just
as she reached the entryway, a key turned in the front
door. Tawni stepped in.

"Mom and Dad were called to the hospital," Sierra
said. "I don't know what's going on."

"Why didn't you call the hospital?" Tawni said,
hanging her purse on the same peg she always used
on the hall coat tree.

"I thought they would call or just come home if
everything was okay."

"What time did they leave?" Tawni asked, heading for the kitchen phone in a huff.

"Around six-thirty."

Tawni dialed the number for St. Mary's written
in chalk on the wall blackboard. She asked for Granna
Mae's room. They waited while it rang. "No one's
answering," Tawni said. "What do you think is happening? Wouldn't a nurse answer it at the station?"

"I guess. I don't know." Now Sierra was feeling pan-
icked. "Do you think we should go to the hospital?"

"Are the boys asleep?"

Sierra nodded.

Tawni held out the phone for Sierra to hear it ring.
"That's the seventh ring. Nobody is there." Hanging
up the phone, Tawni headed for the front door. "I'm
going. You stay here with the boys."

"Call me as soon as you get there," Sierra said.

"I'll try," Tawni said and swished out the door,

closing it hard behind her.

Sierra stood in the entryway next to the full laundry basket. She didn't know what to do. Finally, she reached for her backpack and took it into the office. With supreme concentration, she turned on the computer and began to punch out her report.

Her mind was only half in gear as she waited for the phone to ring. Then, to make sure the phone was working, she reached over, picked it up, and checked for a dial tone. It was working. Sierra went back to her paper. She wrote nonstop for twenty minutes.

Come on, Tawni! Call me! What is keeping you?

Sierra pushed herself to finish the report. It was like walking uphill against the wind. She checked the wall clock every few minutes and picked up the phone twice to call but decided to wait for Tawni.

Her paper was almost finished. Sierra glanced out the French doors at the inky black backyard. It reminded her of the verse she read in Isaiah. Something about "my soul desires You in the night." Sierra sat in the silent room, staring at the phone, praying for Granna Mae.

She forced herself to finish her paper, ran a spell check, and then pressed "print." As soon as she heard the printer kick in, Sierra went into the kitchen and dialed the hospital. It was 10:40, more than an hour since Tawni left. The phone rang in Granna Mae's room. Mom answered it on the second ring.

"Mom, is everything okay? What's going on? Tawni was supposed to call me."

"I know," Mom said calmly. "I'm sorry we didn't call. Why don't you go to bed? We'll be home shortly."

"Can't you tell me what's going on?" Sierra asked.

Mom paused. "We'll be home soon." Then she hung up.

Now Sierra was really stumped. Why couldn't Mom say anything on the phone? Sierra retrieved her paper out of the printer, shut down the computer, and cleared her things out of the office. Then she lugged the laundry bucket upstairs to her room and started to sort clothes on her smoothly made bed. All her T-shirts were in one pile and all the clothes that needed hangers in another pile, while the third stack consisted of her underwear. One of her socks was missing its mate. For some reason, she thought she had seen it in her backpack.

Sierra went downstairs, retrieved her backpack, and brought it up to her room. Then, because she was in a cleaning mood, she dumped its contents out in the middle of the floor and started to sort through all the junk.

The sock was there, but it was dirty. She decided to run down to the basement and toss in another load so her laundry would be all caught up. On her way back up through the kitchen, Sierra decided a little midnight snack would be nice. She popped a piece of bread into the toaster oven and poured herself a glass of milk. The only way to eat toast late at night, according to Dad, was with butter and honey. That had become Sierra's favorite way too.

Balancing the plate in one hand and carefully sipping the milk as she walked, Sierra returned to her room. She sat cross-legged on the floor, sorting through the backpack mess and munching on her toast, trying not to panic over Granna Mae.

In the thick of her sorting frenzy, she heard the front door open. She jumped up and ran down the stairs. "Well? Is she okay?"

Tawni hung up her purse. "What a mess! That has to be the most unorganized hospital in the world."

"What happened?"

"Granna Mae was confused. She got out of bed and walked down the hall."

"With the IV in?" Sierra asked.

"She pulled it out. Then she took the elevator to the lobby and went into the gift shop. She slipped and fell. Mom and Dad have been sitting with her this whole time in x-ray. That's why they didn't call. They were worried about leaving her."

"I thought you were going to call," Sierra said.

"I tried, but every time I went to the pay phone someone was using it. Don't you want to know how she is?"

"Of course I do."

"She broke her foot," Tawni said. "They just started to put the cast on when I left. I think Mom and Dad will be with her another hour or at least until she settles down for the night."

"Is she still confused?" Sierra asked.

"Very. I think the doctor is going to put her on some stronger medication to sedate her."

"When will she come home? Don't you think she would do better here where she would be in familiar surroundings?"

"I don't know what the doctor is going to say. I wasn't convinced the guy even knew what he was doing."

"He isn't her regular doctor," Sierra said, turning to go back to her room. Tawni followed her upstairs.

"Well, I didn't think much of him," Tawni said.

The minute Tawni stepped into their room, she barked, "Aren't you ever going to clean up this disaster?"

"I did!" Sierra protested. Then she glanced around and realized that, even though her side of the room had been cleaned up for about ten minutes, now it was a disheveled mess with clothes on the bed, backpack innards strewn across the floor, and the remains of her midnight snack on her previously tidy dresser.

"You could have fooled me," Tawni said, kicking off her shoes and placing them in her closet.

Sierra jammed most of her loose stuff into her backpack. Then, because Tawni had irritated her, she purposely shoved all her clean, folded clothes off her bed and onto the floor. She climbed into bed, unable to enjoy the fresh, clean sheets, and snapped off her light.

chapter fifteen

THE ROLLER COASTER ON WHICH SIERRA'S emotions had been riding came to a halt Saturday afternoon for a few precious moments. Then, without warning, the ride began all over again.

She was at work and had successfully made it through the first five hours without a mishap. She felt kind of eerie, as if she was just waiting for something to go wrong.

It had been a wildly busy morning. The time flew by. At noon, Mrs. Kraus told her to take a break and get something to eat. A tray of slightly burnt cinnamon rolls were up for grabs in the kitchen, so Sierra picked at one of them. But she had lost her appetite for cinnamon rolls after being around them all morning.

As she sat there, her hands sticky and her clothes smelling like coffee, Sierra felt content. Her job was going well, her dad had made the airline reservations, yesterday she had eaten lunch at school with Vicki and Amy, and this afternoon the sun had come out.

Sierra adjusted the dangling silver earring in her right ear lobe and smiled to herself. She thought of another verse she had read in her speedy journey through Isaiah that morning. "In quietness and confidence will be your strength." Right now she felt a little bit of that quietness and confidence in the Lord. It was very sweet.

Then the roller coaster ride started up again. Mrs. Kraus called into the back room, "Sierra, you have a visitor."

She walked out into the busy shop and glanced around, looking for who it might be. Randy was standing by the cash register.

"Hi," he said. "Do you want to go out tonight?"

Sierra felt her cheeks instantly flush. Several people were staring at her. "Ahh, tonight?"

"Around seven," Randy said. "I thought maybe we could see a movie or something. When do you get off?"

"At four." Sierra realized that Mrs. Kraus was beside her, trying to ring up a purchase on the register. "Oh, excuse me." She stepped to the side.

"Randy—" Sierra began.

"Just say yes," he said, lowering his voice. "Don't make everything so hard, Sierra. We're just friends, right? Friends can go to the movies without it being a big deal, can't they?"

"Is anyone else going?"

"No. Do you want someone else to go?"

"Well ..." Sierra didn't know how to tell him that

she had never been on a date before. She had never been asked, so she had never gotten an okay from Mom and Dad. Her parents had said that when she turned sixteen she could date, but her sixteenth birthday had come and gone without any dating prospects. "Could you do me a favor, Randy?"

"Sure," he said, his crooked smile lighting up.

"Could you give me a call at home sometime after five? I need to check with my parents." Then, because she thought it sounded kind of babyish, she added, "My grandmother is in the hospital, and I'm not sure if it would work out for me tonight."

"Sure. I understand. Now can I ask you a favor?"

"Sure."

"Can you give me your phone number?"

Sierra reached for a napkin and wrote it down.

"Thanks," he said. "Now may I buy a cinnamon roll from you, or do I have to go back and stand in line?"

"I'll get it for you," Sierra said. "With or without frosting?"

"With. Definitely with."

Sierra made sure she was paying attention as she pulled out a tray of hot, frosted rolls and used the wide spatula to scoop one into a container to go. She even plopped a little extra frosting on top before she closed the container's lid. Randy took the roll from her and handed her the exact amount of cash. "I'll call you," he said. With a wave, he was gone.

Sierra let out a tight-chested breath and glanced at

the clock. Her break was over, so she moved on to helping the next customer. None of her coworkers made any comments about Randy. She was thankful for that.

At the same time, she was dying to talk to someone about this major event in her life. She had been asked out on a real date!

As the afternoon continued at a sporadic pace, Sierra had more time to think about this date. She had dreamed about what it would be like when she was asked out for the first time and who the guy would be. But she never had dreamed it would be like this, rather unromantic and so direct. And she never had dreamed it would be with a guy like Randy.

Nothing was wrong with Randy—or so she tried to convince herself. He was valuable "buddy" material. But she had never thought about going out with him. It made her wonder how long he had contemplated asking her out. Did he like her the first day he had met her at school? Or did something spark for him the other day in the cafeteria when she offered her hand in friendship? And if it did for him, why hadn't anything sparked inside of her?

In the midst of wiping off tables and filling the little ceramic baskets with packets of sugar, it hit Sierra that maybe he was doing this out of pity. Maybe he felt sorry for her since she had opened up a little about not having any friends. Sierra jammed a blue packet of artificial sweetener into the white basket and thought,

He can forget it if that's what this is all about. I don't need his sympathy. I would much rather have no dates—ever—than to accept a charity date, especially from someone I thought was my friend!

She held to that course of logic the rest of the afternoon. That is, until she started to walk home and passed the mailbox into which she had dumped her flaming letter to Paul earlier that week. She still regretted sending it. If only she had waited and thought it through a little more clearly. Paul was teasing her, not attacking her.

She had had such strong feelings for Paul when she first met him. For weeks she had prayed fervently for him. And now she had ruined even the little bit of friendship they had had. Maybe it wasn't friendship, but it was something. And it was still there, inside her head.

"Mom," Sierra called out when she entered the house. "Are you home?"

"She's at the hospital," Tawni shouted back from the family room.

Sierra went into the family room, which was being remodeled. Dad had made an entertainment center and had christened it fully operational the night before. The boys were sprawled on the floor playing a video game, and Tawni was labeling some videotapes and filing them in a new tape drawer.

"Make sure you put them in alphabetical order," Sierra said.

"What's that supposed to mean?" Tawni shot her a glance over her shoulder.

"I'm just sure that you'll be happier once everything is in its proper place." Sierra dropped onto the floor next to the boys and asked, "Who's winning?"

"Nothing is wrong with being organized, Sierra," Tawni snapped. "But then you wouldn't know anything about that, would you?" She went back to her task, and the two sisters ignored each other.

"Do you want to play the winner?" Dillon asked Sierra.

"Sure," she said. Then she remembered. Randy was calling at five. "Do you guys know when Mom and Dad will get home?"

"Dad's here," Gavin said. "He's out in the workshop."

"I'll be back," Sierra said, bounding to her feet and hurrying out to the backyard. She found Dad in the dollhouse-looking workshop with goggles on and an electric saw revved at full speed in his hand. She covered her ears and waited for him to notice her.

He reached the end of the board he was cutting and saw her. Dad turned off the saw, flipped up the safety glasses, and said, "You're home! So how did today go? Any adventures to add to Thursday's account? By the way, I've called the people from *Guinness Book of World Records*, and they're considering your experiences for the 'worst first day' page."

"Tell them to find some other klutz to write

about. My dork days are over. Today was relatively uneventful."

"Relatively?"

"I was asked out," Sierra said.

Dad put down the saw and stepped closer to look into Sierra's eyes. He had done that with all his children when they were little to see if they were telling the truth. As they grew older, he continued the gesture. Sierra thought it was his way of reading pains and joys they had learned to bury deeper inside the older they became. Dad always said that eyes were the heart's mirror. "Tell me about it," he said.

"It was a guy from school, not someone I just met at work, if that's what you're thinking. He kind of ate lunch with me one day at school this week. His name is Randy. He came into work and asked if I wanted to go out tonight at seven o'clock. I told him I'd need to talk to you. He's calling at five. What should I do?"

A slow smile spread across Dad's face. Sierra wasn't sure what it meant. "Five o'clock, huh?" He checked his watch. "Leave it to me." He revved up his radial saw one more time before turning it off and placing it on the workbench. Like a man on a mission, Dad whipped off his safety glasses and, with long strides, made his way out of the workshop and toward the kitchen phone. "Yep," he called over his shoulder, "you just leave this one to me, Sierra."

chapter sixteen

"DAD," SIERRA PLEADED, GLANCING AT THE kitchen clock. It was a quarter to five, and Dad stood next to the kitchen wall phone looking ready to "draw" the instant it rang. "You're not going to do anything weird, are you?"

"*Moi?*" he teased.

"I don't want you to do to Randy what you did to Tawni's old boyfriend, Martin," Sierra said.

"Who, Martin the Martian?" Dad asked.

"Are you guys talking about me?" Tawni said, stepping into the kitchen at just the right moment.

"Did Sierra tell you?" Dad asked. "She's been asked out on a real, live date."

"You're kidding!" Tawni said.

"Nope. It's true. Some poor, unsuspecting fellow named Randy asked her out at work today."

"Where did you meet him?" Tawni asked.

"At school. He's just a friend, you guys. I never would have thought he would ask me out."

"It's time you realized what a beauty you are,

Sierra. I'm sure Randy will only be the first in a long line," Dad said.

"Yeah, well I just don't want him to be the last after you get a hold of him," Sierra said, crossing her arms and giving Dad a stern look.

"Oh, you're not going to do to him what you did to Martin, are you?" Tawni asked. It was the first time she had taken Sierra's side on anything in a long time.

"Listen to her, Dad," Sierra said.

"That interview stuff you did with Martin was too much, Dad. Don't do that to this guy. What's his name?"

"Randy."

"Don't do that to Randy. You scared off Martin, and I gained a reputation for being the least accessible girl in Pineville! Don't you remember how everyone made fun of me and said that whoever wanted to go out with Tawni Jensen had to first go out with her father?"

"It didn't hurt you any, and I got a free game of golf and two dinners out of the deal," Dad said. "Besides, that's the kind of reputation I want my girls to have."

"It doesn't have to be so extreme, Daddy," Tawni said, slipping into her mushy side and pleading on Sierra's behalf. "Maybe you could invite him over for dinner or something casual with the whole family. That one-on-one male bonding approach is too severe. Okay?"

Dad thought a minute and said, "I have an idea."

Just then the phone rang.

Sierra looked at the clock: five o'clock right on the button. She looked at her dad and then shot a skeptical glance at Tawni.

"I'll answer it," Dad said. He waved a hand at Sierra and Tawni as if to say, *Don't worry about a thing.*

Sierra bit her lower lip and listened.

"Hello. . . . Yes, Sierra's right here. By any chance is this Randy?"

A short pause followed.

"Nice to meet you, Randy. Hey, before I hand the phone to Sierra, I was wondering . . . ah, Sierra said you two were trying to make plans to do something tonight around seven."

Another short pause.

"Well, if you're interested, we're having pizza here at six o'clock. You're welcome to join us if you would like."

Another pause.

"Okay. Did you want to talk with Sierra? . . . Oh, okay. Bye." Dad hung up. His expression didn't give any clues as to what Randy's answer had been.

"He said no, didn't he?" Sierra asked. "He canceled the whole thing and said he would never bother me again, right?"

Dad's sly grin crept up his face, and the corners of his eyes crinkled the way they did when he was trying not to cry.

"What did he say?" Tawni asked, grabbing one of Dad's arms.

Sierra grabbed the other arm and gave it a yank. "Tell us or we'll pull you apart at the seams."

"What kind of pizza do you ladies want?"

"He's coming then?"

"At six o'clock."

Just then the phone rang. Sierra grabbed it before Dad had a chance to. "Hello?"

"Sierra?"

"Yes."

"Oh, hi. It's me again. I can't believe this, but I forgot to ask where you live."

Sierra let out a nervous laugh. While Dad and Tawni listened in, she gave Randy directions and then asked, "So you don't mind having pizza with my family?"

"Are you kidding? I never turn down free food!" Randy laughed when he said it, and Sierra felt more at ease.

"I'll see you in about an hour then. Bye."

"See you!" he said.

Sierra hung up and turned to face Dad and Tawni with a hint of a smile on her face.

"I told you to leave it to me. I know the way to a man's heart. It's through his stomach. Always has been, always will be. Trust me on this one, girls."

"So what's going to happen when the poor guinea pig arrives?" Tawni asked. "Are you going to lock him in the office and make him sign release papers before they can go out?"

"Noooo," Dad said, giving Tawni a quick kiss on

the forehead and then repeating the gesture on Sierra's temple.

"What are you going to do to him?" Sierra asked.

"You'll see." He headed for the front door and called into the family room, "You guys want to go with me to pick up a pizza?"

"You're going to change, aren't you?" Tawni asked.

Sierra looked down at her light-blue denim jumper and white, short-sleeved T-shirt. "What's wrong with this?"

"You've been wearing it all day, not to mention that you wore it at work."

"So? It's comfortable."

"Sierra, you could at least make a little effort to act like this is your first date. You know, brush your hair or something. You can borrow some of my makeup if you want."

Sierra forced herself to swallow the immediate laugh that came to her. She never had worn a pinch of makeup. Why would she start now? And for Randy of all people. It was a ridiculous thought. But she refrained from laughing because it was one of the most generous and un-Tawni-like things her sister had ever said to her. Tawni rarely shared anything, but especially nothing personal like her thoughts, her clothes, her jewelry, or her makeup. Sierra didn't want to ruin the moment.

"Thanks, but I don't think so. Not for sitting around eating pizza and going out to the movies."

Tawni scrutinized Sierra's face and kept pushing. "A tiny bit of mascara. That's all I suggest. It's your choice."

"Well, okay. I guess so. Just a tiny bit, if it means so much to you."

"I'm only trying to help!" Tawni snapped.

"I know, and I appreciate it. I really do. But just a little bit of mascara, okay?"

Tawni coached Sierra all the way to their room. "You should change into jeans, but not those baggy ones."

"What's wrong with my baggy jeans? They're my favorite."

"They make you look fat."

"They do not."

"Yes, they do. And they look sloppy, like you bought them in the boys department at Sears."

"I did not!" Sierra protested.

They stopped in front of their bedroom door, and Tawni turned to give Sierra one of her I'm-right-and-you're-wrong looks.

Sierra stared right back at her. "I did not get them in the boys department at Sears." Then, lowering her voice and adding a mischievous grin, she stated, "For your information, I bought them in the boys department at Marshalls. They were three dollars cheaper."

chapter seventeen

A T TEN MINUTES TO SIX, SIERRA STUDIED HER
reflection in the antique beveled mirror
above the dresser in their room. Tawni
stood behind her, admiring her own handiwork.
Sierra's hair was pulled back in a loose braid fastened
at the end with a large, wooden clip. She wore no earrings, which made Sierra feel naked. Tawni said they
were too cumbersome. The simple, fresh-faced look
was what Tawni was after tonight.

"Innocence with a pinch of an attitude," she said
while twirling the mascara wand over Sierra's upper
lashes. "That's you to the core, Sierra. You should look
the same on the outside as you are on the inside. Now
hold still. You're not making this easy."

"You're going to poke me in the eye."

"No, I'm not. Relax. I know what I'm doing."

"You're trying to make me look like you, Tawni.
I'm not you!"

"I'm *not* trying to make you look like me."

"So why are you doing this?"

Tawni pulled back and in a curt voice said, "Why do you make it so hard for anyone to treat you nicely?"

Sierra's comeback was "Maybe it's because I'm used to certain people criticizing me rather than complimenting me."

Tawni let the challenge fall to the floor. She went back to running the mascara wand over Sierra's row of eyelashes. "There." Tawni stood back, and they studied the results together. "You look really good," Tawni said. "See what a difference a tiny bit of personal care can make in your appearance?"

Oh, brother! Sierra thought. She still wasn't sure how she felt about being "all dolled up," as her dad called it. She looked at her face without making a comment. Her eyes *did* look larger. They even looked a little bluer than usual. But the freckles sprinkled across her nose made her look more girlish than sophisticated like Tawni. No amount of eye makeup could counterbalance that.

Still, she looked older than sixteen. At least, she thought she did. And Paul had thought so too, when he had first met her in London. He hadn't believed her when she had told him her age.

I wish I was going out with Paul tonight instead of Randy, Sierra thought. *If I was, I'd let you give me the full treatment, Tawni! I'd want to look as fabulous as I possibly could. But I'm not going out with Paul. I will probably never see him again. I should be happy a guy like Randy is interested in me.*

"Well?" Tawni asked. "What do you think?"

Sierra remembered when Granna Mae had stood before this same mirror a number of weeks ago. She had looked closely at her reflection and touched the wrinkles in the corners of her eyes and said something about being twelve just yesterday.

Somehow Sierra felt she was at a milestone too. It was odd thinking that her grandmother had seen her own reflection in this mirror when she was twelve and when she was sixteen and many more times during the five decades that followed. It was strange to think about Granna Mae being sixteen.

"Aren't you going to say anything?" Tawni prodded.

"It's weird."

"Oh, thanks a lot."

"I'm not talking about the makeup. I'm saying it's weird to think we have only one chance to cross the bridge from childhood into adulthood. And then we can never go back. This feels like one more step across that bridge."

Tawni looked startled at Sierra's comment. "Since when did you turn into a philosopher?"

"Don't you ever think about stuff like that?"

"Yes, of course I do. I never thought you did."

"I do sometimes. Like now."

Tawni put away her makeup bag and selected a bottle of fragrance from the collection on her dresser top. She squirted a tiny bit into the air above Sierra's head. "I think you're a light, sweet fragrance kind of person. Do you like this?"

Sierra took a whiff of the air. It didn't smell like Tawni. It was more like a fresh shower scent. "Yes, I like that."

"Then close your eyes, and I'll scent your hair."

"You'll what?"

"Close your eyes." Sierra did, and Tawni gave her hair several squirts. "There. Now you're ready. Except for your outfit, that is."

"Let's make a deal," Sierra said. "You got to do all the stuff above the neck, so I get to pick what goes on below the neck."

Tawni shrugged. "Suit yourself." She put the perfume bottle back where it belonged and picked the hairs from her brush.

Sierra sorted through the heap of clean clothes on the floor and pulled out a striped T-shirt and a pair of baggy jeans. Ignoring her sister's small sounds of disapproval, Sierra carried her clothes down the hall to the bathroom, where she could change in peace.

Dad returned with the pizza before Randy arrived. Sierra could hear Dad and her brothers in the kitchen. As she headed downstairs, the door opened, and Mom came in, looking tired.

"How's Granna Mae?" Sierra asked, meeting her in the entryway.

Mom took a second look at Sierra. "You look wonderful! Did you do your hair?"

"No, I was Tawni's project for the afternoon. I kind of have a date tonight."

Mom's tired lines vanished, and her face brightened. "You didn't tell me! Does Dad know?"

"Of course. He invited Randy over for pizza with the family. He should be here any second. Do I look silly?"

"Sierra Mae Jensen," Mom said, taking Sierra's hands in hers. "You look adorable. You have no idea how attractive you are."

Just then they heard heavy footsteps on the front porch and the sound of a male clearing his throat. Then the doorbell chimed. Sierra and Mom squeezed hands and exchanged silent giggles with their facial expressions.

"I think it's for you," Mom whispered, slipping into the kitchen.

Before Sierra could answer the door, Gavin and Dillon charged in from the kitchen, fighting over who was going to open the door. They both jerked the old doorknob at the same time, and the knob fell off in Dillon's hand.

"You broke it!" Dillon yelled. "Dad, Gavin broke the doorknob."

"I did not! You did!" Gavin shouted back, pushing his brother.

"Hey, you guys," Sierra yelled above their shouting. "Cut it out!"

Dad came around the corner from the kitchen

with Mom right behind him, both loudly asking what the problem was. At the same time, Tawni appeared at the top of the stairs and hurried down to find out what was going on.

"I'll need a screwdriver," Dad said. "Dillon, run out to the workshop and find a Phillips head and a flat head."

"But I didn't do it!" Dillon protested.

"I didn't say you did. Just get them for me, will you? Hang on there, Randy," Dad called through the closed door. "We'll open the door in just a minute here."

Sierra felt herself wilting in the midst of all the frenzy. Randy certainly could hear all the commotion. She wouldn't blame him if he turned around and ran all the way home. Everyone was talking at once, trying to solve the problem. Dillon returned with three different sized screwdrivers, and Mom was saying a missing piece probably had fallen on the floor. She got down on all fours and started her safari in between everyone's legs. Gavin joined her and immediately found a dead bug he wanted to save.

"Try opening it with just the screwdriver," Tawni suggested. "You don't need to put the handle on to open it. The same thing happened before with the bathroom doorknob, remember? Granna Mae just uses a coat hanger and sticks it in there."

"I know how to do this," Dad said, sounding irritated. "I did grow up in this ancient house, you know." He pressed something inside the doorknob hole with the flat-head screwdriver. It clicked, and Mom popped up her head, colliding with Dad's elbow.

"Ouch!"

"You okay?"

"Open the door!"

"Stand back, you guys!"

"Wait a second. Let me stand up."

"Look out for my bug!"

The door opened, and six eager faces smiled to greet Sierra's date. No one was there.

Sierra thought she was going to cry.

"Hi guys," a voice behind them said. They all spun around and saw Wes, Sierra's oldest brother. Randy was standing next to him. "I found this poor guy out on the porch. Does anybody claim him?"

"I do," Sierra said, feeling her cheeks turn flaming red.

Mom rushed over to hug Wesley and give him a big kiss. "You didn't tell us you were coming home from college this weekend."

"What? Do I need to make reservations now or something? Maybe that was your problem," Wes said to Randy. "You didn't call ahead. They only open the door if you call ahead. But now you know my secret: sneak in through the back door."

Everyone laughed, and Sierra said, "Everybody, this is Randy. Randy, this is my family. I forgot to warn you about them."

More laughter.

Randy just stood there with a dazed look on his face.

"Let's attack the pizza while it's still hot," Dad suggested, motioning with his arm that they should all follow him into the kitchen. As he passed Randy, he said, "So, do you like anchovies, Randy?"

"Uh . . . well, not too much, sir."

"Oh, too bad," Dad said.

Sierra stepped over beside Randy and said, "Don't worry. He didn't get anchovies. He hates them. He's just teasing you. He probably got pepperoni or something. Don't worry."

"Oh, I'm not worried," Randy said, his half grin barely inching up the side of his jaw.

Sierra smiled her best smile at him. But Randy looked worried. Very worried.

chapter eighteen

ONCE THE TROOPS WERE SEATED AT THE DINING room table, eating pepperoni pizza off paper plates and sipping Pepsi from the cans, Randy appeared to relax more.

"You look like that guy in that rap group," Gavin said to Randy. "Are you that guy?"

Randy shot a glance at Sierra and said, "I don't think so."

"Are you in a band?" Gavin wanted to know.

"No."

Gavin looked disappointed.

"My dad used to be, though," Randy said. "He played the drums."

"That's pretty cool," Dillon said. "Do you play drums?"

"A little. I play piano some too."

"Oh." Apparently piano wasn't nearly as cool as drums when it came to Dillon's choice of instruments.

"What does your dad do now?" Mom asked.

"He's a scientist."

"Da' mad Mr. Science-Head," Gavin said in a deep voice with his arms raised over his head and his hands hanging down like a gorilla.

"It's a cartoon," Dillon explained on behalf of his little brother.

"We could have guessed," Wes said.

"What kind of scientist?" Mom asked.

"He's sort of a geologist."

"Sort of?" Tawni challenged.

Randy looked at Sierra, and then with a hopeful expression he said, "He's actually with a team of men and women who are searching for Noah's ark." Randy scanned everyone's face looking for feedback.

"Fascinating," Dad said. "Wouldn't it be something if they found it."

Randy looked relieved. "Some people think that's weird. He also works with a team of scientists who study Mount Saint Helens, but he's really into the Mount Ararat project."

"Is that where you got that really great coat you wear to school?" Sierra asked. "You told me your dad bought it in Nepal."

"He brought it back for me last year when he was over there."

"Does your mom work outside the home?" Mom asked.

"She teaches third grade at the Christian school."

Sierra glanced around and felt relieved that things were going much more smoothly than they had at first. The conversation continued until all the pizza was gone. Dillon challenged Randy to a game of "Agitated Alligator," his new video game, and Wes said he would play the winner.

"Do you mind?" Randy asked Sierra. She could tell he was dying to play the game.

"What time do we need to leave for the movies?" Sierra asked.

"It depends on what you want to see," Randy said. He handed his empty plate to Sierra's mom as she moved around the table collecting them. "Thanks," he told her with a smile. "Great dinner."

"Yes, I slaved all day over a hot pizza oven. Glad you liked it."

"What do you want to see?" Sierra asked, trying to regain Randy's attention.

"It doesn't matter to me. As long as it's good and clean."

"Randy," Dillon called from the family room, "it's all ready."

Randy looked at Sierra. She was trying to decide if she should be upset. Everyone else had stepped out of the dining room, and she knew she could say whatever she wanted. "Oh, go ahead. We don't have to see a movie. We can just hang out around here."

Randy smiled. "You don't mind?"

She shook her head. "Not this time."

"Randy!" Dillon called again.

"I owe you a movie," Randy said.

"I know," Sierra said. "And I won't let you forget it, either."

Sierra showed Randy into the family room, where Wes was already at his place at the controls. "I'll show you how to work this thing," Wes said.

"Oh, I think I can manage it," Randy said.

Wes handed him the controls and said to Dillon, "Look out, little buddy! When they act cool like that, they're really master video game champions trying to cover up their expertise."

"What's 'expertise'?" Dillon said.

"Watch and learn," said Randy, making himself comfortable on the floor and pushing the start button. Sierra had a feeling she wouldn't see him again the rest of the night. She went into the kitchen for a drink of water. Pepperoni always made her thirsty.

Tawni was at the sink, helping Mom with the few dishes that had accumulated during the day. She turned to Sierra and said, "I can't believe you're letting him do that!"

"Let who do what?"

"You turned your date over to your brothers. Those guys will play video games all night long. Don't you care that he jilted you like that?"

"Actually, no. I think I feel more comfortable with my first date being like this."

"This isn't a first date. Not when he dumps you for a runt!"

"Tawni," Mom said gently.

"This is a first date," Sierra said firmly. "This is how *I* do first dates. And I happen to like it this way."

"Well, I sure wouldn't," Tawni said.

"It's not your first date," Mom said to her older daughter. "Although I remember yours being a bit of a disaster. Didn't he take you to a restaurant that was out of business?"

"His dad told him it was a good place. They just hadn't been there for a year."

"I remember that," Sierra said. "You ended up at a Dairy Queen or something, and you were all dressed up with your hair fancy and everything."

"We still had fun," Tawni said with a slight pout.

"And I intend to still have fun tonight," Sierra said. "Anyone for a round of Trivial Pursuit?"

"Great idea," Mom said. "I'll tell Dad to set it up."

"I get Wes on my team," Tawni said.

Within twenty minutes, four teams were steeped in battle over the Trivial Pursuit board. Sierra and Randy were the team in the lead, followed by Mom and Dad. Gavin and Dillon were last, and they pooped out after half an hour and went back into the den to watch a video.

The game went on. At nearly ten o'clock, Sierra reached her hand into the popcorn bowl and drew another fistful to her mouth. Randy rolled the dice, and she said, "Okay, this is it. Game point!"

Randy moved their marker to a hot-pink square, and Wes pulled the question card from the box. "Oh, perfect!" he said, reading the question to himself. "You'll never get this, Sierra."

"Let me see," Tawni said, looking over Wesley's shoulder. "I have no idea what the answer is. You'll never get it, Sierra."

"Just read it," Mom said.

"Okay. For the game, the question is, what was Elvis Presley's middle name?"

Sierra let out a groan, but Randy immediately answered, "Aaron."

Tawni and Wes exchanged poker-faced glances. "Is that your answer? It must be a team decision."

Sierra looked at Randy. "Aaron? Are you sure?"

Randy nodded.

She couldn't tell if he was right or not. He had come up with some really bizarre and very wrong answers earlier in the game. She didn't know him well enough to know if he was faking it or not. Sierra drew in a deep breath. "Okay," she said. "I'll go with Aaron."

"I don't believe it!" Wes said, slapping the card onto the table. "It's right."

Randy slapped Sierra a high five. "We're the victors!"

"All right! How did you ever know that?"

"I told you my dad used to be in a band. I didn't say it was a Christian band."

They all pitched in to clear the table and carry the empty popcorn bowls and glasses to the kitchen. Everyone sat around talking for another half hour or so before Randy stood up to leave.

"I better get going," Randy said. "Thanks for a really great evening. Bye, everyone. Nice meeting you all."

Sierra's family said good-bye to Randy, and she walked him to the front door. Dad had fixed the door-knob. Still, Sierra opened it carefully. "Thanks for coming over and everything," she said. "It really was a fun night."

"This was the best first date with someone I've ever been on," Randy said. Then looking over Sierra's shoulder to make sure no one was listening, he added, "Can I tell you something?"

"Of course."

"This was my first date of any kind."

"You're kidding! Mine too." She started to laugh, and Randy joined in.

"It'll make the second date a whole lot easier," Randy said. "I still want to take you to the movies. Maybe next weekend."

"Sure. That would be fun."

"Well, good night," Randy said, giving her a crooked smile.

She held up her hand in a casual wave and said, "See you at school Monday." He left, and she carefully closed the door behind him before returning to the kitchen.

"Well, did he kiss you?" Wes wanted to know.

"Of course not! We're just friends. And you want to know something? He said it was his first date too."

"It seemed as if he had a good time," Mom said.

"Once he got over the initial shock of our crazy intro-
duction."

"Thanks, you guys, for 'double-dating' with me,"
Sierra said.

"Any time," Dad said. Then, turning to Tawni, he
asked, "Well, was that better than the Martin the
Martian disaster?"

"It depends," Tawni said.

"On what?"

"On whether or not he asks her out again. That
will be the test."

chapter nineteen

SIERRA HAD A HARD TIME FALLING ASLEEP THAT night. She felt as if she should think about Randy, what a fun guy he was, and how great the evening had gone. But she was thinking about Paul, wondering what it would be like to have him come over for pizza with her family. How well would Paul do at Trivial Pursuit? Would Paul have known Elvis's middle name?

She kicked at the covers and turned onto her side. *What does it matter? Why am I thinking about him? My letter to him was enough to frighten anyone away. I can't believe I wrote all those things.* She thought back on how she had ended the letter, first by accusing him of using the word *sincerely* when she knew he wasn't. And then by signing the letter so stupidly. *What was it I wrote? "Irritatedly yours?" No, "very irritatedly." Why did I do that?*

With a groan she flipped over onto her back and stared at the dark ceiling. She remembered the notes in her journal about saying "forgive me" and "thank you," and the wisdom of using them often in her youth. She wanted to say "forgive me" to Paul. Even if he still thought she was an immature nerd, she didn't care. It was better than living with the memory of the unbridled words she had put into writing and mailed without thinking.

Sierra thought of how Granna Mae had told her last summer that whenever she had a big decision to make or if something was bothering her, she would bury it for three days and not think about it at all. Then, if on the morning of the third day, she found that choice or concern was alive, it would be evident God had resurrected it.

At the time, Sierra didn't understand what Granna Mae meant and had thought her grandmother was rambling. Now Sierra understood. If she had buried that letter right after she wrote it, then when she went back and looked at it three days later, her emotions would have calmed down, and she would have been thinking more clearly. That's what she would do next time. But for now, she needed to apologize.

In the stillness of the room, Sierra began to make her plan. Sunday afternoon she would write a letter of apology to Paul, and then she would call Katie and Christy to tell them that her dad had made her airline reservations.

As she began to doze off, feeling much more settled, Sierra remembered one of her recent verses from Isaiah. *With my soul I have desired You in the night.*

She thought that was about the most romantic thing anyone could ever say to someone else. She whispered it aloud to the Lord. "With my soul I have desired You in the night, Jesus. Do You become tired watching me bumble things? Sometimes I get stuff right. Like tonight. That was a wonderful first date. Thanks for making it that way. Thanks for my family."

Sierra thought again about the thank-you, forgive-me quote. It seemed that with the Lord, as with all her important relationships, the words she said most frequently were "forgive me" and "thank you." She thought of how much better she would feel once she said "forgive me" to Paul.

But her eyes popped open when she remembered she had crumpled up his first letter and tossed it away. She wished she hadn't. Once again the three-day resurrection principle would have been helpful.

The next morning, as Sierra dressed for church, Mom tapped on the bedroom door. "Sierra, may I come in?"

"Sure."

"I just called the hospital to check on Granna Mae and guess what? The doctor was in her room, and he said we can bring her home this morning. Would you like to help me pick her up? He wants us to be there right away so he can go over some instructions."

"Of course I'll go with you. Hang on. I'll be ready in a minute."

Dad took the rest of the family to visit the church

Tawni liked in Vancouver while Mom and Sierra drove to the hospital.

"I'm relieved to have her come home," Mom said. "I know it will be a lot of work at first, but I'm glad I can count on you and Tawni to help out. She has her left foot in a cast, and I think they're going to give her a cane. She should be able to walk upstairs if we help her. I think she'll be glad to get back in her room."

The doctor was waiting for them and had a list of printed instructions. One page was on caring for a patient with a broken bone, and the other was for a patient recovering from gall bladder surgery. Sierra wished they had one dealing with an elderly person who was losing her mind.

"How are you feeling?" Sierra said, leaning over and giving Granna Mae a kiss on the cheek. "Did the doctor tell you that you get to go home today? This is earlier than we thought. You're doing so well!"

Granna Mae smiled and said, "Only a few like him are left in this world. Don't let him slip away."

Sierra assumed Granna Mae meant the doctor, who was standing right there. Granna Mae's favorite doctor, Dr. Utley, who had performed the operation, was still on vacation. Tawni hadn't thought much of this other doctor, but apparently Granna Mae did. Either that or she was rambling again.

"We'll send up a wheelchair," the doctor said as Mom signed some papers.

A nurse who had been standing nearby suggested,

"You might want to make a trip to the car first to find a place for all these flowers."

"I'll take them," Sierra said. "I can probably do it in a couple of trips." She reached for the first gorgeous bouquet and read the card tucked in the plastic holder. It was from some of Granna Mae's neighbors. The next one was from her friends at Eaton's Pharmacy. There was a live plant from her friends at church. Sierra tried to balance the two bouquets and hold a vase in her hand. She got a good grip on them and was able to carry them all the way to the car only to discover it was locked.

On her second trip, she brought the keys and unlocked the car. All the flowers fit in the backseat just right, with enough room for Sierra to perch next to them on the way home.

She jogged back into the hospital, thinking about how great it was going to be to have Granna Mae home. She was glad Granna Mae had come through the surgery okay. Even with her broken foot and her memory problems, she was still alive.

When Sierra had met Paul, he was returning from his grandfather's funeral in Scotland. They had talked about how close they each were to their grandparents. Sierra had always considered Granna Mae a good friend as well as her grandma. Paul had seemed to understand that.

Why am I thinking about Paul? I have to move on. I have other friends to think about—Randy, Amy, and

Vicki, and maybe even Tawni in a unique way.

Sierra remembered she had invited Tawni to go to California with her over Easter. She still wasn't sure why she had done that. The subject hadn't appeared again on Tawni's lips, so Sierra had determined not to bring it up either. Tawni had probably forgotten about the invitation. In two weeks, Sierra would be on her way to visit her good friends.

Until then, she had friends to eat lunch with at school, a possible date to the movies next weekend, many cinnamon rolls to serve, a dear Granna Mae to care for, and an apology letter to write.

When Sierra stepped back into the room, Granna Mae was already in the wheelchair, and her face was looking much brighter. "One more flower, Lovey!" she said. "I want to take all my daffies home with me. He was such a dear young man. Kept me company most of the evening after you left last night, Sharon."

"That's nice," Mom said, gathering Granna Mae's personal belongings from the rest room.

On the tray table was a small white vase with a single yellow daffodil. Sierra hadn't noticed it before. It almost seemed like a small decorative touch that had been served with the breakfast. She wondered if someone from the hospital had brought it from his garden. Maybe the young man Granna Mae was rattling on about was a volunteer who had taken a shine to her and kept her company last night while Sierra and her family were all at home, busy playing Trivial Pursuit.

"Are we ready?" Mom asked, preparing to push the wheelchair out the door.

Granna Mae turned to the doctor and held out her hand. He grasped it, and she held his. From her lips came a gracious "Thank you." She thanked each of the nurses who came to say good-bye too. Sierra grabbed the final daffodil and followed the procession down the hall.

"Looks like you were pretty popular around here," Sierra said as two more nurses looked up from the central nurses' station and waved their good-byes. "I don't know about you, Granna Mae," Sierra teased. "Making friends everywhere you go, strange men bringing you flowers in the night ..."

The small gift card attached to the daffodil vase rubbed against Sierra's thumb as she marched in Granna Mae's exit parade. Sierra glanced at it. The sight of the bold, black letters made her stop in her tracks. In a mixture of cursive and printing, the card held only two words: "Sincerely, Paul."